the Iciest SIN

the Iciest SIN

M

H.R.F. KEATING

THE MYSTERIOUS PRESS
New York · Tokyo · Sweden · Milan
Published by Warner Books
W A Time Warner Company

Copyright © 1990 by H.R.F. Keating
All rights reserved.

Mysterious Press books are published by
Warner Books, Inc., 666 Fifth Avenue, New York, NY 10103

A Time Warner Company

Printed in the United States of America
First Printing: December 1990
10 9 8 7 6 5 4 3 2 1

Library of Congress Cataloging-in-Publication Data

Keating, H. R. F. (Henry Reymond Fitzwalter), 1926–
    The iciest sin / H.R.F. Keating.
       p.   cm.
    ISBN 0-89296-427-8
    I. Title.
    PR6061.E26I25   1990
    823'.914—dc20   90-6093
                                           CIP

Designed by Giorgetta Bell McRee

Blackmail is the iciest sin.
—Rebecca West

ONE

Tell me, Inspector, who is the most dangerous woman in Bombay?"

Inspector Ghote felt a green wave of coldness swirl up in him.

The most dangerous woman in Bombay? He did not know at all. There were plenty of women he had encountered in his years as a police officer who could be called dangerous. The mistresses of notorious antisocials, smugglers of drugs, madams of brothels. But the most dangerous? It seemed to him an unanswerable question.

Yet, no getting round it, an answer was being demanded of him. And by none other than Mr. Z. R. Mistry, Additional Secretary in the Department for Home, a man who held in the palm of his hand the careers of every police officer in the city.

He looked at the lean, large-nosed face implacably regarding him, chin forcefully jutting prowlike, eyes behind the heavy spectacles blinking and blinking.

Despite the urgent need to find some plausible name to put forward, Ghote's mind went back, magnet-drawn, to when, earlier that day, the Assistant Commissioner, Crime Branch, had told him Mr. Mistry wished to see him "on a private matter."

"A strictly private matter, Inspector. Understand? I know nothing about it, nor am I wishing to know."

And then there had been the error he had made when he had arrived at Mr. Mistry's residence at the exact appointed hour, seven in the evening. The servant, a morose-looking individual in a floppy white uniform, dusting cloth over his shoulder, and with a truly terrible squint disfiguring his face, had opened the door to his ring at the bell. And immediately he had said to him—that appalling squint had shunted everything else from his head— "Inspector Ghote to see Mr. Z. R. Mistry." While all along as he had made his way to the flat's block, Marzban Apartments up on Malabar Hill, high above the sweating city, he had kept telling himself that, since this was so insistently "a private matter," whatever he did he must not mention his police rank.

And now, to pile new embarrassment on old, there was this unanswerable question: "Tell me, Inspector, who is the most dangerous woman in Bombay?"

"Sir, I do not think that I am able to say."

It was a bad beginning. But there seemed to be nothing for it but the bald truth.

"No, Inspector? Well, I am not altogether surprised. The lady—her name is Miss Dolly Daruwala—conducts her affairs in a distinctly clandestine manner. She resides even, I am sorry to have to tell you, in this very building. Up on the twentieth floor, the penthouse apartment, one quite beyond my own means."

Mr. Mistry stared gloomily down at the floor at his feet.

Ghote, waiting to be told more, thought that however dangerous this Miss Dolly Daruwala was, her name in fact meant nothing at all to him, beyond that like Mr. Z. R. Mistry's own it must be from the Parsi community. That extraordinary band of people had long ago come to India from Persia and had eventually established themselves in all sorts of key positions in Bombay. But why was this lady dangerous?

Mr. Mistry, however, seemed to have gone into an almost permanent trance of deep thought, looking down at the beautifully polished black shoes he wore with his traditional Parsi garb—Ghote had been a little surprised to find him in it—of white, shirtlike dugla with bows in place of buttons and loose white trousers.

"Sir," Ghote ventured at last, "please, what for exactly are you dubbing this lady as dangerous?"

"Blackmail, Inspector," Mr. Mistry shot out, coming back from his reverie with a small start. "Blackmail. Miss Dolly Daruwala may well be the most practiced blackmailer Bombay has ever seen."

He gave Ghote a somber look from behind his heavy spectacles.

"Blackmail," he said. "Perhaps the most hateful crime, short of murder, that is to be found. I once read of it described as the iciest sin, Inspector, and I think that puts it very well."

The iciest sin. Yes, Ghote thought, it did put it well. To seize on some crime or misdemeanor, an indiscretion even, and to threaten the person who had committed it with exposure unless they paid and paid, it was something that required an icily cold mind to conceive and persist in. An icily cold mind.

But Mr. Mistry could not have summoned him here simply to tell him the name of this blackmailing lady. If he wanted action taken against her, he did not need to call an officer of Crime Branch to come and see him. The Commissioner himself—it was well-known—had a meeting every week with the Additional Secretary. Then, too, there were the Assistant Commissioner's ominous mysterious words at his briefing: *A strictly private matter—I know nothing, nor am I wishing to know.* What had he been summoned here to be told then? What?

Waiting again, patiently as he could, till the powerful figure who had summoned him to his private address at this unorthodox hour chose to enlighten him, Ghote took a discreet look around. For all that Mr. Mistry had implied that his flat was much less opulent than the penthouse above occupied by Miss Dolly Daruwala, the room that he had been shown into by that squinting servant was loomingly impressive. Tall-backed armchairs of dark rosewood were grouped here and there with little intricately carved heavy tables beside them. Against the walls large glass-fronted cabinets in the same heavy wood glinted with pieces of delicate china and silver. High above them dark oil portraits of Parsis of bygone days, dressed like Mr. Mistry in traditional white duglas but wearing as well old-style glossy, black-lacquered Parsi hats, puggrees, looked down with high-toned disdain. In a corner a nearly life-size statue of a half-naked man bent under the weight of the round world on his shoulder had set into that burden a clock gravely ticking away the hours.

At last Ghote tried a little questioning cough.

But it served only to produce from the Additional Secretary a long, almost dreamy spate of casting-back reminiscence which, as it wound onward, simply added to Ghote's bewilderment.

"You know, Inspector, I had the happiness myself to be brought up in a household that practiced to the full all the traditions of our community. The regular visits to the temple, the proper prayers said at the proper times, the navjote ceremony that initiated me into our faith, declaring my allegiance to the cutting short of quarrels, dedicating myself to the self that is holy, the wearing of the dugla, as I wear it now, and the sacred kusti. You know what that is, the kusti, Inspector?"

Ghote did know, and was quick to say so.

"It is a small ceremonial garment, yes? Worn round the waist?"

"Made always from lamb's wool, Inspector. Hand spun. In seventy-two separate strands. I can see my grandmother now twirling her spindle, letting the thread slowly drop as it ran from the hank of wool in her hand, turning her wrist rhythmically to and fro. One is invested with the kusti at one's navjote, you know, a ceremony which in my case was attended, so I have been told, by no fewer than two thousand members of our community, all afterward our guests."

"Yes, sir," Ghote said, though he felt his words lacked the enthusiasm Mr. Mistry must expect.

But when were they going to get down to business?

"Yes, our traditions and ceremonies have always meant a great deal to me. For what they symbolize, Inspector. The life that our community dedicated itself to from the time we arrived in India, and our mobed, our high priest, proved by slipping a jeweled ring into a pitcher of milk, proffered to demonstrate how crowded the kingdom was, that we would enrich the land but occupy little of its space. For, too, that prayer we offer in front of

the sacred fire in our temples: 'O God, we praise Thee by offering
good thoughts, good words, good deeds.'"

Yes, yes, Ghote thought. You Parsis have been fine fellows
always. But when am I to learn what it is I have been brought
here for?

And Mr. Mistry had not finished yet.

"Yes, Inspector, and I think I can say that good deeds are what
we have offered to India from the very start. Why else are so
many of Bombay's finest thoroughfares named after Parsis: Dr.
Dadabhai Naoroji Road, Dr. Cawasjee Hormusjee Street, Sir
Jamshedji Jeejibhai Road, Madam Cama Road, Jamshedji Tata
Road? You know the first Indian to be knighted by the British
was a Parsi? And the first Indian Fellow of the Royal Society was
another? And the first Indian, too, to be appointed to the High
Court?"

Yes, Ghote thought again, but what is all this leading to?

He realized then that the stream of reminiscence had at last
dried up. Mr. Mistry was once more contemplating his polished
black shoes.

Then he lifted his head and looked at Ghote with his ever-
blinking, weak Parsi eyes.

"However," he said, "I fear I have been somewhat led astray.
The point I was attempting to make was that when a community
has so much to be proud of, such fine and ancient traditions,
anything that would tarnish that name is, if it is at all possible, to
be avoided."

The eyes behind the heavy spectacles ceased their blinking and
gave Ghote a glance of shrewd assessment.

"You understand, of course, Inspector, I will never connive at
anything that grossly transgresses the law as it stands."

"Yes, yes. Of course, sir."

"But, nevertheless, there may be occasions . . ."

Again he shot Ghote a sharp glance.

"Inspector," he said, "I have a relative, a distant cousin . . ."

Once more he fell silent. And once more began again.

"Well, I realize I cannot withhold his name from you, though

I must insist that anything I tell you goes no further. No further at all in any circumstances."

"Oh, yes, sir," Ghote hastened to put in. "You can be sure to one hundred percent that whatsoever you are saying will remain altogether locked inside my breast."

"Very good. Well, this relation of mine, a distant cousin only, you understand, but a cousin nevertheless, is one by name Burjor Pipewalla, by profession a tax consultant."

Now Ghote thought he was beginning to understand. Mr. Mistry had taken pains to tell him about "the most dangerous woman in Bombay," the blackmailer who had the penthouse flat at the top of this very building, and now—at last—he was adding that he had a relative who was a tax consultant. And a tax consultant more often than not was, simply, a man who made a good deal of money out of showing people with even more money how to get out of paying the taxes that they properly owed. And that was a field wide open to blackmailing.

"Yes, sir?" he asked as neutrally as he could.

"Well, some weeks ago this young man came to me and told me that—that certain papers from his office had been made away with by this Miss Dolly Daruwala I was telling you of. She had pretended to consult him about her financial affairs over the course of a number of visits, and during the last one she had abstracted these papers. I do not know exactly what they are, and I have been careful not to ask. But I understand from young Burjor that, should they fall into the hands of the income tax authorities, the consequences might be very grave."

Mr. Mistry gave a little tight cough.

"Now, the point is," he went on, his voice slowing with every word, "that Burjor, rather foolishly, has been paying Miss Daruwala over the months various sums of money in the expectation of receiving those papers again. An expectation, as you will no doubt not be surprised to hear, in which he has been deceived. Now at last he has come to me, knowing my work is largely concerned with the police, to ask if there is anything I can do discreetly to put an end to Miss Daruwala's activities."

"Well, sir," Ghote said, "the procedure in such cases is clear.

Any person willing to stand witness against a blackmailer is granted the protection of being named in court only as Shri X or Shrimati Y, as the case may be."

"Yes, yes, Inspector. All that is well-known to me. But have I, in such approaches as I have been able to make, been able to secure one single person willing to take on the role of, as you say, Mr. X or Mrs. Y? I have not."

"Except only your cousin, Mr. Pipewalla?"

Mr. Mistry sighed.

"That is what I was endeavoring to put to you earlier, Inspector," he said. "It is out of the question that any member of our community should appear in court in a matter of this sort if it can at all be avoided. Out of the question. Whatever precautions are taken, something may leak out and the name of the Parsi community be irretrievably blackened."

"Yes, sir."

Little point in saying to such a person as Mr. Z. R. Mistry that this was a risk that ought to be taken.

"So, Inspector, it is here that you come in."

"Myself, sir?"

For all that he had come to realize that it was for this that he had been summoned to the Additional Secretary's residence at this unofficial hour, Ghote felt abruptly as if iron manacles had been clamped on to him. He was at a loss to know what exact services he was going to be required to undertake. But all too plainly there was some plan Mr. Mistry had in mind for him. And whatever it was, it could only mean trouble of the deepest sort.

"Yes, Inspector," Mr. Mistry went on, his eyes momentarily ceasing to blink and his prow chin jutting forward another quarter of an inch. "I have given the matter considerable thought, and I have arrived at what I believe is the only possible solution."

"Yes, sir?"

"Inspector, Miss Daruwala is accustomed to conducting her insalubrious affairs in her flat. And here, in a few days' time, my young cousin is due to go to pay her another large sum, and to plead with her once again for the final return of those documents which could do him so much harm. I have decided that this meeting must be witnessed, in secret, by a reliable police officer."

"But, sir, if there is no possibility of the complainant coming to court . . ."

"No, no, Inspector. I have told you, that is out of the question. However, the lady, for all her nefarious activities, is by no means well versed in the law and its ramifications. She is of comparatively humble origin. I do not suppose she even went as far as to pass Junior Cambridge. So I am altogether certain that if she was to find her dealings with young Burjor had been witnessed by a police officer, and one who would resist any attempt at bribery, she would thereafter agree, were it suggested to her, to leave India forever."

"Yes, sir," Ghote said.

What Mr. Mistry had told him was probably true, he reflected. A woman without much knowledge of the law, if such a conversation as she was likely to have with this tax consultant had been overheard by a police officer, could be frightened into leaving the country altogether. But—

But that would be blackmail. Nothing less.

The thought, as he arrived at it, seemed to empty his mind of everything else. How had this come about? How was it that he was suddenly being asked to connive at that exact icy sin that Mr. Z. R. Mistry himself had only minutes earlier condemned so wholeheartedly? Could that be right? And yet, in a way, it did seem right. It was, after all, the means by which a blackmailer, one with no doubt many other victims also under her grasp, was to be defeated.

So ought he to agree to it?

At once he realized that there was no question of agreeing or not agreeing. Not really. He was being given orders by the Additional Secretary in the Department for Home. And, though those orders concerned "a private matter," it was altogether clear that he was expected to obey. And if he should refuse? If here and now he stated that he could not be a party to any attempt at blackmail? Well then, at the least, he would find himself swiftly posted away out of Bombay. Into the Armed Police perhaps, or to some hundred percent backwood. There to spend the remaining years of his service.

He suppressed the groan that rose up in him.

"Sir," he said, "what is it exactly that I am to do?"

TWO

What Mr. Z. R. Mistry said that he wanted done redoubled Ghote's fears and doubts.

He wanted Ghote to get keys made to Dolly Daruwala's flat from impressions in soap which, he said, Burjor Pipewalla had obtained on the last occasion he had gone there. Then he required Ghote to enter the flat surreptitiously before the time of his cousin's next blackmail payment, to conceal himself somewhere and at the right moment emerge and confront Dolly Daruwala.

"But, sir . . ." Ghote said. "Sir, entering that flat in the manner you have mentioned is H.B. only. It would be an offense against Indian Penal Code."

"Yes, Inspector," Mr. Mistry replied urbanely. "You are right. It is housebreaking, of course, technically a criminal offense. Nevertheless I am asking you to commit it."

"But, sir, I am a police officer. I cannot do it."

Mr. Mistry's eyes behind his spectacles blinked yet faster.

"Inspector," he said, "you were represented to me as being an officer who could be relied upon in the situation we have in front of us."

"Well, yes, sir, I am happy to hear. But—but, sir, was it understood that I was to be asked to commit an offense?"

Mr. Mistry regarded him bleakly. In the silence of the big, darkly furnished room, the slow ticking of the clock in the round ball of the world on the statue's shoulder seemed to take on the ominous note of a bomb waiting to explode.

"No, Inspector," Mr. Mistry said at last, his voice chill. "Naturally, when it was a matter of such confidentiality, precise details were not mentioned. However, what I understood from my sources was that you were—how shall I put it?—an officer who would not make trouble, who was not in a position to make trouble."

"Yes, sir," Ghote said.

He knew now his worst fears were being justified. He had been picked to go to the Additional Secretary, that figure of power, on this "private matter" not because of any special talents or qualities he might have. He had been selected because someone had judged him to be in too weak a position to object to whatever he might be asked to do.

And their judgment was right. How on earth could he resist this pressure? To do so would be to ensure he got that posting to the depths of the mofussil, where there would be no school for his son to go to now that he was past simple reading, writing, and arithmetic, where his wife would languish, away from the life of the big city she was used to. There, too, he himself would be on a minimal pay scale, only to be enhanced by accepting such bribes as were going. And that he would not do. And, perhaps worst of all, he would no longer be a member of Crime Branch, an officer dedicated to the uncovering of serious wrongdoing, the task he had believed from his earliest days was his dharma in this life. Instead he would be little more than a mere administrator. At best the putter-down of occasional riots, at worst only someone who, against all odds, would strive to maintain good order and discipline in some forgotten police thana.

"So I can take it, Inspector, that you will not, in fact, make trouble?"

"No, sir. No, I will not."

Well, he thought, now I have succumbed to some blackmail myself. Or if it is not blackmail to one hundred percent, it is something not far off from it. I have been made to do what in the inmost middle of my heart I know I should not do, and I have been made to do it by a threat.

And the fact that it is in one good cause does not at all make it easier to bear.

He arrived home some half an hour later, leaden-hearted. But as he tapped on the door to have it unbolted, he heard a joyous shout from inside. It was Ved. "Dada is back. Dada is back." Big though the boy is now, he thought, he is still at heart a child only. Pleased to see his father. Delighted with simple pleasures.

The bolt was scraped back, the door flung open.

"Dada, Dada. Where have you been? I have something to ask. Important-important."

Ghote felt the weight of his gloom lifting.

He smiled.

"Well, what is this that is so important? Some problem with homeworks, no?"

"No, no, Dada. Homeworks are not at all a headache. You are knowing I am standing first in almost every subject. No, this is much, much more vital."

"Vital? All right then, tell me."

"Sit, sit, Dadaji. You must be paying full attention."

Ghote sank into his chair and kicked off his shoes, already feeling that life was not quite so terrible as it had seemed while he was riding his motor scooter home.

"Well, I am listening."

"Dada, what I am wanting most of all in the world is home computer."

"Home computer?"

Ghote experienced a sense of swirling bewilderment. Was this the boy who, not months before it seemed, had been able just only to master the multiplication table? And now he was saying he wanted a computer? How could he know how to work such a thing? It was something far beyond his own capacities. And how could he even think of getting something that no doubt was appallingly costly?

That last question was soon answered.

"Listen, Dadaji, they are selling home computers, smuggled, on the footpath at Flora Fountain. But you know what Aii is always saying about she is hating smuggling, and she has forbidden me to go there, although I have saved and saved enough of money. Nearly."

Ghote sat up straighter.

"Well, if your mother has forbidden," he said, "then that is end of matter."

He felt relieved. Somehow he did not relish having a son who owned that mysterious, modern-age thing, a computer. And now, thanks to Protima's prejudice against smuggled goods, which after all was a sensible and proper attitude, there would be no question of this plunge into the twenty-first century taking place within his own home.

Ved was looking furious, misty-eyed almost with tears. But he would get over it.

"But, Dadaji, you must tell Aii that-all is nonsense only. Or, better-better, you must tell her the home computer I will get is not at all smuggled."

"Well, beta, that is out of question. I do not know for how little they are selling such things at Flora Fountain, but certainly in any pukka shop they will be costing altogether more."

"Yes, yes. That I am knowing. But what it is you must do is pretend smuggled home computer is properly imported one."

"Oh, yes?" Ghote could not restrain a smile at the wild suggestion. "And why should I do a thing like that? Deceiving my own wife, isn't it?"

Ved, kneeling in boyish supplication in front of him, took on a sudden look of intransigent determination.

"Because," he said, his voice low and urgent, "if you are not helping, then I would tell Aii that our TV, which you were letting her believe had been bought properly from Vision Radio and Computer Service, when it was Vision Radio Service only, was also one smuggled article."

Ghote felt a sharp sinking of dismay. It was true that when he had at last agreed to the acquiring of a television set, he had,

when one of his fellow officers had told him he could get a
smuggled item at less than half price, succumbed to temptation.
And, worse, one day he had jokingly boasted to young Ved
about the little piece of deception.

Then a swirl of outrage rose up in him.

"My son," he said, directing to Ved all the ferocity he was
capable of, "never let me hear you try to obtain something in that
manner ever again. You know what they are calling it? They are
calling it blackmail. Blackmail. That is the iciest sin. The iciest
sin. And there is one only way to deal with same. It is what one
damn fine Englishman, Duke Wellington by name, was saying to
a lady when she was threatening to write in some book his
naughty doings. He was saying, 'Madam, publish and be
damned.' And that is what anyone who is asked to cow down to
blackmail must be saying also."

His ferocity had the desired effect. Young Ved's face at his knee
went pale.

"Yes, Dadaji," he said, and, scrambling up, he raced out of the
room.

And Ghote sat there thinking that not an hour earlier he had
altogether failed to say to Mr. Additional Secretary Mistry
"Publish and be damned."

Standing in his uniform outside the towering white block of
Marzban Apartments, waiting till the chowkidar guarding the
entrance should be distracted long enough for him to get past
unobserved, Ghote felt burning in his pocket the set of false keys
he now possessed to Dolly Daruwala's penthouse flat.

At length one of the residents emerged with his wife from the
lift inside, and the chowkidar hurried over to where their driver
had brought their car and opened its door. Ghote left the patch
of deep shadow in which he had been lurking and slipped into
the building. He took the stairs rather than the lift, anxious at all
costs to avoid being seen.

But it was a long, long climb.

And, when he neared that twentieth-floor flat at last, he
thought, would his keys turn out to be the right ones? He had

been doubtful from the very moment when Burjor Pipewalla in the somber surroundings of the library at the Parsi Ripon Club had handed him the piece of soap into which he claimed he had pressed both the flat's door keys.

"Damn fine piece of luck for me," he had muttered breathily, leaning toward Ghote in a waft of chewed betel nut odor. "Bloody woman is always putting down her key-bunch just as soon as she is getting home. On a table beside a vase of flowers she has there. That I was often noticing, so it was easy for me to get impressions in this soap."

Ghote had formed an instant dislike for the fellow. He was a podgy young man of about thirty, his pale face decorated with a thin little moustache under which a cigarette grew bright and dull alternately. Hands folded over a rubber-ball potbelly, he had made no attempt to get up from the dark cane-backed armchair in which he was reclining as Ghote had been shown in.

"Yes," he had said as soon as Ghote had discreetly identified himself, "I was not at all wanting you to come to my office, and there is generally no one about here in the library at this time of the afternoon. Now, you know what you have to do, yes?"

"I was receiving instructions from Mr. Z. R. Mistry."

"No names, no names, you fool. And for God's sake sit down. I don't want every word I am saying to be heard all over the club."

It had taken an effort not to reply that the library, with its ranks of ancient-looking, meticulously numbered books behind their glass doors, with its portraits of Parsi worthies of bygone days and its heavy furniture, was, as Burjor Pipewalla himself had pointed out, altogether deserted.

After his few bare words of explanation the tax consultant had handed over the thick envelope containing a piece of soap. Glancing at it, Ghote had recognized from the faint odor of limes that it was a piece of Liril. The two impressions in it showed every sign of having been made in haste.

"Well," Burjor Pipewalla had demanded, "can I be relying upon you to be in place in that flat tomorrow. Miss Daru— The person we are speaking of is always playing bridge on Wednesdays. She returns home at about eleven in the night, and I have insisted on an appointment for that time. I trust that you will make sure of hearing each and every word she says."

He had looked up then, the eyes in his pale face hard.

"And you will forget thereafter whatsoever you yourself have learned. Understood?"

"Mr. Mistry was fully explaining to me."

At that, Burjor Pipewalla's full lips had tightened in abrupt petulance. But he had said no more.

Wearily Ghote hauled himself up the last, ill-lit flight to Marzban Apartments' twentieth floor. On the landing he stopped and listened. No, no one was coming up behind him. He moved over to the door of the flat, slipping the two false keys from his pocket.

What if they would not turn in the locks? The Muslim mechanic he had gone to in Bapu Khote Cross Lane in the Pydhonie area, an old record-sheeter whose name he had found in the files, had looked at Burjor Pipewalla's two impressions with contempt written on every line of his wrinkle-cut face. But that might have been only because he was not happy about making false keys for a police officer, suspecting perhaps some attempt to entrap him.

It had been then that, with sudden gray weariness, Ghote had known he would have to use what he had put together about the man from Records and had learned at the Modus Operandi Bureau.

"Listen, bhai," he said. "There are many, many things against you that we are knowing. You want to be charge-sheeted with making keys for that big Byculla housebreaking last year? You are thinking we could not find evidence enough if we are wanting? Or there is job at that posh flat in Cumballa Hill last March only?"

The old Muslim had glared at him in fury. But it had been impotent fury. A fury of a kind he knew well himself. He had felt it when Mr. Mistry had applied his form of blackmail in the flat at the foot of this very block.

Had the Muslim, in revenge, even mismade the keys? No, he would not have dared. Or would he?

He took a step nearer Dolly Daruwala's door and put his ear to one of its gleaming teak panels.

And heard sounds.

Voices were talking, quite loudly and with some argumentativeness, it seemed. But whose could they be? He listened again. All men's voices. Nothing that sounded like Dolly Daruwala. So was she, as Burjor Pipewalla had said, still playing her regular Wednesday evening game of cards? Could she have invited some people to wait for her? Then the voices ceased, and there came, absurdly, other voices, ones he at once recognized, singing voices, softly chanting, "Vico . . . Turmeric . . . Ayurvedic . . . Cream . . ." The television. The damn woman must have left her television on. Perhaps, in fact, she did so deliberately. Mr. Mistry had said she kept no servant. Too many secrets to take the risk of prying eyes. So quite likely when she went out for the evening she put on the television to scare away possible housebreakers.

Like himself.

Wryly he took the first of the Muslim's keys and tried it in the door. It scraped home a little stiffly, but eventually he got it to turn. The second key gave him no trouble at all.

He pushed the door gently open.

Inside, he found Dolly Daruwala had left almost all the lights on, and, yes, the television was continuing to pump out advertisements in one of the rooms leading off the hallway where there was, as Burjor Pipewalla had said, a table holding a big creamy-white fluted vase, resplendent with flowers.

He looked at his watch. Only just past ten. He still had plenty of time to find the best place to conceal himself. Carefully he set out to explore. The whole flat seemed to be every bit as luxurious as the rich blooms on the table beside the door had indicated. In the drawing room a huge flowery Amritsar carpet covered most of the floor. Low western-style chairs and a sofa, pink in raw silk with dark green cushions, gave a very different impression from the last Parsi residence he had been in, Mr. Z. R. Mistry's apartment down below. A coffee table with a white marble top held a heavy silver cigarette lighter he saw as deliberately flouting the Parsi edict against employing sacred fire for smoking, together with a copy of a well-known scandal magazine called *Gup Shup*. On the walls were some Chinese scrolls, framed in gold, and a picture of the British Princess Di's wedding. Parsis were mad about the British Royal Family.

He glanced in at the bathroom, every bit as opulent as the rest of the place. The bath and basin had gold taps. Dozens of bottles of scents and lotions, mostly with Western names and smuggled in, no doubt, crowded its shelves. And all, he thought, if what Mr. Mistry had told him was right, bought out of the proceeds of the lady's blackmailing operations. Only the kitchen was somewhat bare. No doubt Dolly Daruwala neither cooked for herself nor dared have a servant to cook for her.

Finally he went to the bedroom beyond the drawing room, where, according to what Mr. Mistry had said, Burjor Pipewalla had seen Dolly Daruwala's safe. In it lay, he had gathered, not only the documents that could land the plump tax consultant in prison, but papers that many a wealthy person must feel as a hair-hung sword above them, held back only by regular payments to the most dangerous woman in Bombay.

He spotted at once where the safe must be. There was a single painting in the room, a copy of that one in Europe of the lady smiling mysteriously—what was it called, the Mona Lisa—and as soon as he went over to it he saw that it could be swung back on hinges. And behind it, set into the wall, was a small but first-rate Godrej safe.

Mr. Mistry had said that Dolly Daruwala had gone to this the first time his cousin had come to pay her the "fine" she had told him she felt it was "her duty" to impose instead of the one that a court would levy, or the prison sentence that would be laid down if the papers she had "accidentally" picked up at his office should fall into the wrong hands. Then, letting him see that in her handbag there was a little, gleaming, stubby pistol, she had put the thick bundles of notes he had brought her into the safe and had handed over to him the papers. Only to let him know one month later that she had felt it her duty, again, to retain copies.

Ghote could see that scene in his mind's eye. He felt a dart of pity, even for the unpleasant Burjor Pipewalla.

But more urgent considerations awaited. Where amid all this luxury was he to hide so as to be sure of hearing every word when Burjor Pipewalla arrived? And where could he himself be sure of not being found when Dolly Daruwala got back, no doubt a few minutes before that eleven o'clock appointment?

He went over the whole of the flat in his mind. The bathroom? No, Dolly Daruwala was altogether likely to go in there as soon as she reached home. The kitchen? Well, it looked unlikely that she would enter that, but hiding there he would not be able to see what was happening in the drawing room.

So it would have to be the bedroom. He tried stepping into the tall fitted cupboards that lined one whole wall. Sari after sari, in the pastel shades that Parsi ladies favored, would provide ample cover even if Dolly Daruwala put something away. But, again, among all that shimmering silkiness, although the wood-work was unexpectedly flimsy for such a luxurious place and he would hear well enough, he would be able to see nothing of what was happening in the rest of the flat.

But then he looked at the bed, smooth under a cover of glossy green. It was placed so that, if the door of the room was ajar, anyone lying on it, or under it, could see the greater part of the drawing room beyond. And there seemed to be space enough beneath.

He looked at his watch once again. There was more than enough time before eleven o'clock. But on the other hand, Dolly Daruwala might return early. Best to take no risks. He got down onto the floor and carefully slid his body past the flounces of the silky bed cover.

When his eyes had become accustomed to the gloom under-neath, he found himself confronting, right under his nose, two gray coils of dust and fluff. At once he feared for the cleanliness of his uniform. Leaving home to come to Marzban Apartments, he had contrived, filled with a vague sense of shame at what it was that he was to wear the uniform for, to slip out with it bundled over his arm while Protima was in the kitchen. He had then changed down at headquarters, intending to reverse the process when his unpleasant task was over. Now if the dust beneath the bed left marks on his uniform that defied brushing he would have some embarrassing explaining to do.

But at least by raising an inch or so the flounce of the bed cover just in front of him he had a good view of the drawing room, where Dolly Daruwala was likely to conduct her interview. And if she came in to go to her safe he had only to turn his head and lift the flounce at the side to be able to see what she was doing.

He lay listening to some more inane advertisements issuing from underneath the prettily embroidered dust-cover that hid the television. "Rich creamy Milkmaid . . ." Then, "Liril—with the fresh tang of limes." Well, in the end there had not been much fresh tang of limes left in the piece of soap he had had to blackmail—yes, that was what he had done, no getting past it—the old Muslim locksmith into using to make those keys.

In the drawing room the television advanced to the news in English, droning on with the more or less statutory item about the Prime Minister, a speech extolling a certain Dr. Edul Commissariat, who had recently returned from America bringing some invention that was going to end all India's ills. No doubt, he thought, allowing himself a jet of venom in compensation for the unpleasantness he was embroiled in, they were even now showing yet once again the shot of Dr. Commissariat stepping out of his plane in Bombay that they had shown half a dozen times already since his arrival.

He found his thoughts had turned again to the business of blackmail. What damn cheek it had been in Ved to threaten to tell Protima the secret of his TV set purchase. Perhaps he should have beaten him. But, no, the boy was good at heart, and doing so well at school. Besides—the thought suddenly came back to him—had he not as a boy himself once tried some blackmailing? A hot flush of shame welled up in him at the recollection. He must have been nine, in Standard IV. And one day he had happened to spot Adik Desmukh, big Adik, stealing one of the girls' pencils. How he had delighted in threatening to tell Masterji. It had given him much more pleasure than the one anna Adik had handed over as the price of silence. And that had been the only payment. Because somehow he had soon been overwhelmed with shame, not at having extracted the coin, which he had actually thrown away in disgust, but at the secret pleasure he had got out of having a big boy like Adik Desmukh in his power.

Well, Ved's sin had not been as icy as his own. By no means. So let it rest. And at least the boy had not tried to repeat his tactic.

From the television he became aware the newsreader had moved on from the Prime Minister. She was recounting now the details of a big strike in Bombay. A prominent labor leader was being quoted.

Oh, yes, he thought, that fellow I am very well knowing. Every sort of a mischief monger, and he does it for money. Employers hand him over fat bribes to get their mills back to work. How else has he acquired his big house out at Juhu? The foreign car he is not ashamed to drive to protest meetings in? What else is he doing but practicing blackmail? Or at the least extortion. Not one hundred percent as nasty, but bad—

His thoughts screeched to a halt. Above the ongoing tones of the newsreader there had come, distinct as the sharp tap of a gecko lizard, the sound of a key in the flat's door.

Already.

THREE

Lying beneath Dolly Daruwala's bed, a gray roll of fluff gently oscillating to his breathing just in front of his face, Ghote did not doubt that the keys he had heard inserted in the flat's door meant that its owner had returned much earlier than expected from her bridge evening. He foresaw trouble. If Dolly Daruwala was to go here and there about the flat until Burjor Pipewalla came to plead with her for the return of his incriminating documents, then it was not beyond the bounds of possibility that something would eventually give away his own presence. And, Mr. Mistry had said, Dolly Daruwala carried a pistol in her handbag.

But, to his sharp surprise, immediately after he heard her drop her bunch of keys onto the table in the hallway—Burjor Pipewalla had been right about that invariable habit, it seemed—her voice came floating into him.

"Come in, come in. Let us discuss this all, just in a friendly manner."

Immediately he knew that she was bringing to her spider's web a new victim. But whoever it was made no response. Then a moment later, raising the green flounce of the bed cover, he saw the lady herself walking into her drawing room from the hall in a way that indicated her victim-guest was following.

Dolly Daruwala was not a pretty woman. He could well

understand how, coming as she did according to Mr. Mistry from one of the poorer families in the Parsi community and thus being as a young girl presumably without any substantial dowry, she had failed to acquire a husband. She was fat, if not hugely so. But there was about her a heavy, settled solidity that must have been with her from her earliest days. Her face, in particular, had an unhealthy puffiness out of which jutted incongruously the sharp beak of her nose. But for all her lack of feminine grace, she was dressed with as much elaboration as if she were a film star at the height of success. Her sari, worn in the Parsi manner across the right rather than the left shoulder and drawn up over her head, though in plain pastel color, a rose-pink, was of rich silk. Around her fat-encircled neck diamonds glittered. Her podgy little fingers were clustered with rings. And even from a distance he could hear her breath coming in short gasps.

With a quick movement she slid from her arm the cobra-skin handbag she carried and plunged her hand into it.

The pistol, he thought. Can she have spotted me? Will she dare to use it?

But what she withdrew from the bag was a little blue plastic vapor spray. She held it to her lips and twice squirted a relieving cloud into her mouth.

Ah, Ghote thought, an asthmatic. No doubt from childhood also.

Now she turned to the person she had led in.

"Come," she said. "Come. Please sit."

And, to Ghote's astonishment, who should walk slowly into his view, leaning heavily on an ornate cane, a small briefcase tucked under his arm, but the man he had only a few minutes before heard the Prime Minister speaking about on television. Dr. Edul Commissariat was the Parsi scientist who had returned to India to set up a superconductor laboratory.

Was he, too, then a victim of the most dangerous woman in Bombay? Surely not. It was impossible. He must himself have misunderstood the situation. Dr. Commissariat must be just someone Dolly Daruwala had known in the past. After all both of them were Parsis, and had not last week's *Sunday Observer* said

that Dr. Commissariat came from comparatively humble surroundings? Perhaps the two of them had been childhood friends,
and now that Dr. Commissariat had returned to India Dolly
Daruwala was taking advantage of the old association to lay claim
on a distinguished person.

But the first words the scientist uttered put an end to that
notion.

"No, madam, I will not sit."

The words had been spoken with complete coldness. With
evident enmity.

Then, after all, Dr. Commissariat must be one of Dolly
Daruwala's victims. But how? How? How could it possibly come
about that such a distinguished man, such a good man—had he
not returned to help his country when, they said, his invention
could have made him five times over a millionaire in the United
States?—had become entrapped in this spider's clinging threads?
What could he have done to let it happen? He had been away
from Bombay, away from India, for years. So what could Dolly
Daruwala have found out about him that had forced him to come
at her beckoning to this lair of hers?

"Just as you like," Dolly Daruwala said in answer to his cold
words. "It makes no difference to me whether we discuss this in
a friendly way or with abuses."

"There is nothing to discuss," Dr. Commissariat shot back. "I
have come here with one purpose only. To demand the return of
those papers you stole, whenever it was that you did, from my
poor dead cousin's parents."

"And what right have you to demand? Let me remind you.
What you call 'those papers' is a thesis that you had half
completed when your brilliant cousin, Feroze, died. And you,
you were quick to pay a condolence visit, like a kite swooping
down, just as soon as tradition permitted, after the dusmoo day,
all those years ago. And there, under pretense of going through
his papers for his parents, who knew no more about your physics
science than they knew about the other side of the moon, you
exchanged his thesis for the one you yourself had been working

at. And with that thesis of Feroze's you got to America, to Harvard or whatever they call it, and all your name and fame."

To yet greater astonishment Dr. Edul Commissariat did not deny the charge.

"Yes," he said. "Oh, yes, you do not need to remind me of that. Of the disgraceful action a young man took, mortified because when he and his cousin had tossed a coin to decide which of them should pursue which line in the theses they were about to begin, mine had turned out to be, whatever its initial promise, almost certainly a blind alley. I have not forgotten what I did, nor will I as long as I may live."

"Never mind all that," Dolly Daruwala said, beginning to puff asthmatically once more. "What you did was absolutely a disgraceful action. And you should be exposed. It is right that you should. What is it it says in the Vendidad, that holy scripture you perhaps still believe in? Something like vermin, pests, and snakes are to be eliminated, yes? It is years since I went to the fire-temple. Well, you should be eliminated, you forger, and I will see to it that you are."

"Oh, yes, you are right. If the newspapers were to get hold of this, it would see me eliminated. But it would not be myself personally. It would be the elimination of the scientist to whom the Government of India has offered a laboratory, something that will give this country a source of energy perhaps to end forever the poverty so many of its citizens still suffer."

"Always trying to make yourself out some great soul," Dolly Daruwala retorted. "Well, you are no such thing, my friend. You are nothing but a cheat and a liar. And it will give me much pleasure to let the world know it."

And then she spoiled the high tone.

"Unless you are ready to pay me. One lakh was the sum I suggested."

A lakh of rupees, Ghote thought. As much or more than I would earn in three or four years. No wonder she is owning such a posh flat.

"No," Dr. Commissariat answered. "No, I will not give you so much as one paisa. But you will hand me back that wretched half-finished thesis in my young man's handwriting that could do me and my country, our country, so much harm. You will. Now."

"Just because you are asking?" Dolly Daruwala laughed.

"Yes, just because I ask. But I ask on behalf of the thousands, the hundreds of thousands, whose lives may be made more bearable from my work."

"Well then, if you are so concerned for all those dalits and low-caste good-for-nothings, it is quite simple. Pay me my lakh. Straightaway, then I will give you your stupid papers—they are here in my safe now—and that will be the end of the matter."

"Except that you will have made a copy of them. I know how people of your kind conduct their nasty business."

Dolly Daruwala gave a curt laugh.

"Well, perhaps I have made a copy," she said. "Perhaps it, too, is in my safe, and perhaps I would have kept it and given you back only your original. I do not pretend to be a saint, unlike some people. But if you have to go on paying till the end of your days, what would that be to you? You can make lakhs and crores from this invention of yours. Wasn't I reading and reading about it and you both until I was sick of the sight of your name?"

"Only, I have agreed not to exploit my discovery in America for what I could make out of it. I have agreed to bring it to India, for the benefit of my fellow countrymen."

"The fellow countrymen you did not care one jot for in all the years you were living your fine life in the States."

"Yes," Dr. Commissariat said, his voice suddenly less deter-mined, "you are right again. I did live in America heedless of those I had left behind, in poverty by the million. But mercifully I was reminded by a visitor from Bombay of what members of our community—Parsis like yourself and myself—had done for their fellow men in the past. People like Sir Sorabji Pochkha-nawala, who created the first truly Indian banking chain—you must know the story of starting in that room with just two chairs in it—or Jamsetjee Tata, who created the whole Indian steel industry, or Ardeshir Godrej, who from being a simple repairer of surgical instruments went on to set up an industry giving work to thousands of his countrymen of all creeds and castes. Of them and dozens of others who, just one Parsi to every five thousand Indians, made such contributions to the nation. Their stories taught me where my duty lay, brought me back here."

"Oh, too good. But do not be thinking that all that 'Good thoughts, good words, good deeds' cuts any ice with me. You say you know what those who practice my nasty business are like. Well, let me tell you the truth of it. How do you think a girl like myself, fat and wheezing even from a baby, disliked by one and all, how do you think she could make her way? I will tell you. By keeping her eyes open, even as a child, and—"

And at that moment a secret fear Ghote had had ever since Dolly Daruwala had returned seized him, the ridiculous idea that, because characters in films and stories hiding like himself always loosed forth a tremendous sneeze at a critical moment, he, too, was bound to do the same. He did not actually feel a sneeze coming on. It was more that, lying there hearing such extraordinary revelations, he could not help thinking that a sneeze ought to give him away. So moment by moment he had become overwhelmed by the fear that he was going to betray his presence there under the bed.

And that brought on, worse by far than a desire to sneeze, a ferocious attack of cramp. A heavy suitcase, one of two he had found in his hiding place, digging into his side made any movement to ease his throbbing leg impossible. Tears came into his eyes. He bit his lip to suppress a gasp of pain. He ground his teeth together and endured.

But through his misery he still just managed to take in what Dolly Daruwala was saying.

"Yes, there was nothing in the world I wanted more than a geometry box like one my big brother Behram had, and I knew all too well no one was going to give an ugly child like myself even an ordinary pencil box. Then one day I caught Behram and some of his friends smoking, and in a moment I saw how I could get my geometry box."

She gave a sharp pounce of a laugh.

"You remember my parents," she said. "Altogether good, religious Parsis. Fire worshipers, as people call us. Smoking was an abomination to them. So all I had to do was to ask Behram to give me that geometry box, and say I would tell if he refused. He did not like it. He did not like it at all. But what could he do? Yet even then in the end it was Behram who got the praise. For being so kind to his little sister, always so bad-tempered."

"Well," Dr. Commissariat replied, "I don't doubt you were driven to the—the profession, if you can call it such, in which you appear to have been so successful. But nevertheless a time must come when you allow other considerations to weigh with you. And that time is now. I ask you again, I ask you in the name of our community, in the name of all the poor of India, to return those papers."

"And I ask you," Dolly Daruwala flung back, "for the sum of one lakh. Cash. Now. I hope you have had the good sense to bring it."

And then, to Ghote's appalled dismay, this fine character who, he had thought more than once as he had listened to his exchanges with Dolly Daruwala, fully matched up to the British Duke Wellington and his "Publish and be damned" abruptly caved in.

"Very well," he said. "Yes, I have brought the sum you requested. So let us be done with the business. Give me those papers, and let us never see each other again."

"Ah," Dolly Daruwala replied, with so much satisfaction that it was altogether audible to Ghote still wrestling with his cramp beneath the bed, "I knew you would see sense. They always do in the end."

"Then get it over with," Dr. Commissariat snapped.

Now they will come in here to the bedroom, to the safe, Ghote thought. Will I be able to keep silent?

The pain in his leg seemed to be easing a little, but he knew it could return, perhaps even more sharply, at any instant.

Hastily he lowered the green flounce he had been holding up. In the now stifling dark he strained to catch every least sound. He made out by the faint squeak of the door being opened wider that Dolly Daruwala had come in. Then he heard her go walking round to where the picture of that Italian or French Mona Lisa hung, her sari swishing silkily. Behind her, he picked out Dr. Commissariat's heavier steps. Weary dejection seemed to sound in every one of them.

But that picture. Had he replaced it exactly right?

Apparently so.

Cautiously lifting the edge of the bed cover by his side, he was able to see Dolly Daruwala now. She had her handbag, with no doubt her pistol in it, over her left arm. He could see that she had taken the precaution of reopening its clasp. Tightly grasped in the fingers of her left hand she had, too, the briefcase Dr. Commissariat had brought with him. It looked big enough to hold a lakh, say, ten packets of a hundred hundred-rupee notes each. Or perhaps Dr. Commissariat had managed to buy somewhere in the Kalbadevi area, at the customary premium of twenty rupees, a quantity of the hard-to-find five-hundred rupee notes.

With her free hand Dolly Daruwala now swung back the Mona Lisa picture. Then, though he could not see what exactly she was doing, any more than Dr. Commissariat just out of his sight at the rear would be able to, he guessed that she was twisting the numbered dial of the safe this way and that.

In a moment he heard a faint clunk as the safe's lock was released. He saw Dolly Daruwala lean backward, tugging at the heavy little door.

Behind her Dr. Commissariat spoke again.

"Even now," he said, "will you not relent?"

"Come," Dolly Daruwala answered sharply. "Forget all that nonsense."

Afterward, Ghote was to recollect that he had then been aware of a sudden swift scraping sound. But at the time he was momentarily mystified to see, an instant later, an inexplicable shaft of silver seeming to arrive from nowhere at the top of the rose-pink sari he had been observing so intently. There had been, too, an odd little noise, which, again later, he thought must have been a single choked squeal of breath.

But what he did see, beyond mistaking, after just a moment more, was the body of the most dangerous woman in Bombay falling to the floor with a single heavy thud. Then he realized that the silvery shaft he had not been able to account for was, in fact, the blade of a sword. Twisting his head farther up, he saw that its handle was the handle of the ornate cane Dr. Commissariat had been leaning on as he had entered the apartment. A sword stick, a gupti.

But it still took him time—perhaps in reality hardly a second—to take in properly the fact that Dolly Daruwala had been killed. And by none other than that good, even noble, man, Dr. Edul Commissariat. It was probably, he thought, looking back on it all, only when he heard the words Dr. Commissariat pronounced, a sort of epitaph, that he had realized exactly what it was that had taken place.

"'Vermin, pests, and snakes are to be eliminated.'"

It was the sentence from Parsi scripture that Dolly Daruwala herself had quoted in contemptuous bitterness to this victim of her blackmail.

FOUR

Something prevented Inspector Ghote from immediately hauling himself clear of Dolly Daruwala's bed and arresting her murderer. It might even have been, he was to think looking back on the whole extraordinary episode, no more in the first few instants after the blackmailer's body had thudded to the floor than the mere difficulty of getting rapidly out from underneath that shiny green affair and onto his feet to confront Dr. Edul Commissariat in a manner proper to a police officer.

But soon enough he was to realize that what, in fact, was keeping him hidden there among the rolls of dusty fluff was a quite different decision he had taken almost without conscious thought. A different decision and a far weightier one.

He had rapidly come to feel, to believe absolutely, that the Parsi scientist was right to have made away with Dolly Daruwala. She had been calmly proposing to prevent him using this superconductor invention of his to pull the mass of his fellow countrymen out of the desperate poverty in which so many of them seemed to be sucked. That alone, set aside all the other victims icily tortured over the years, was sufficient reason, if ever there was reason enough, to condemn her.

Nor could there be any doubt, Ghote soon saw, that her death had been premeditated. Dr. Commissariat had given her a clear

31

chance—more than one even—to think better of her purpose.
Then, when she had scorned him that final time, he had put into
action a plan he must have made almost as soon as she had first
telephoned him with her demand.

The thought of this had come to him abruptly with the vivid
recollection of seeing on television, more than once, the Parsi
scientist arriving in Bombay. Then, plainly, he had in no way
needed to lean on a cane. So he must have taken to using that
sword-concealing gupti as a first step in a carefully worked out
scheme. He had never had any intention of paying the lakh he
had brought in that briefcase. The bundles of notes had been
there only to induce Dolly Daruwala, if all appeals failed, to open
her safe. Then, having given her that final chance, he would be
ready to eliminate the vermin, pest, or snake, which she undoubtedly had been. How ironic it must have seemed to him when she
herself had quoted those very words.

That the scientist had acted with all that premeditation was
soon confirmed. Ghote heard him walk quickly back into the
flat's drawing room and, a moment later, return.

Risking lifting once more the edge of the shiny bed cover, he
saw that what Dr. Commissariat had done was to fetch Dolly
Daruwala's silver cigarette lighter. It took hardly ten seconds for
him to open the lighter's underside, to thrust it into the open safe
and let the fuel in it pour out. A moment later a flick of his
fingers produced a spark that sent the whole contents of the safe
up in flames. All those swords that had perilously dangled over so
many heads, all the soft chains.

As soon as it was clear that nothing in the safe would escape,
Dr. Commissariat carefully wiped the silver lighter with his
handkerchief before pulling the gupti sword out of Dolly
Daruwala's inert body and resheathing it. Then he quickly
stooped, retrieved his briefcase, and walked out of the flat.

For perhaps a minute more, even two, Ghote lay on under the
bed, letting the consequences of his decision not to arrest the
man who had killed Dolly Daruwala slowly flood into his mind.

First, he had acted in a manner totally contrary to all his rooted
beliefs as a police officer. He had with his own eyes witnessed a

crime, the worst of crimes even, and he had done nothing. He was appalled by that. Yet he found he still believed he had been right. Were there, then, sometimes circumstances when it was not a fault to take the law into one's own hands? Plainly Dr. Commissariat, who from even the little he had heard him say was beyond all doubting a good man, believed that was so. He had believed it, and more, he had not hesitated to act on that belief.

So was he himself not right to take the same attitude? To learn from that example put so startlingly in front of him? Perhaps he was. No, almost certainly he was. This was a time, perhaps the only time he would ever know, when there was something that overrode his duty as a police officer. The solemn oath he had solemnly taken.

Next, there was now in his mind, to stay there forevermore, the fact that Dr. Commissariat, that man it was hardly too much to call a great soul, had in fact committed murder. It would even be possible for he himself now—the notion flitted through him like a monstrous joke—to levy blackmail on this noble figure.

Finally he realized that if at any time anything needed to be done to protect this man who had committed murder, then he himself was now obliged to do it. He felt run through him a sense of dread, of almost holy dread.

Slowly, as if some intolerable weight was settling down on him, he shuffled his prone body out beyond the edge of the bed and staggered, cramp-bruised, to his feet.

Then he set himself to think more practically. Already he would have to start acting on Dr. Commissariat's behalf. Before long, one way or another, Dolly Daruwala's body would be found. Had Dr. Commissariat left anything in the way of a clue behind him?

He concentrated fiercely. No, the scientist had almost certainly done nothing in the flat that would betray him. He had come to it with the clear intention, if it had to be, of killing Dolly Daruwala. A man of his intelligence would know all about fingerprints. Had he not taken pains to wipe that lighter? So he would have been careful the whole time he had been in the flat to touch nothing. Nor would he have left anything behind. He had himself seen him remove both his briefcase and the weapon. No immediate fears there then.

But what about himself? It was as important that no one, bar Mr. Z. R. Mistry, who had sent him here, should ever know he had been in the flat at the time Dolly Daruwala had been done to death. But had he been as careful as Dr. Commissariat?

Again he thought. Conscious when he had first come in that he was committing a crime—what a petty offense housebreaking was set against what he had just seen—he, too, had, without even thinking about it, taken every care to touch nothing.

Methodically he retraced his actions from the moment he had stepped inside, tucking his two false keys back into his pocket, till when he had lowered himself to the floor here and slid under the silky green flounce of Dolly Daruwala's bed. And, no. No, he was certain. He had touched nothing. And, thank goodness, his uniform seemed to have stayed clean.

But there was yet another person involved. How had he come not to have thought of it before? Burjor Pipewalla, tax consultant, was due to present himself at the flat at almost any moment.

He looked at his watch.

No, not quite at any moment. It seemed there was almost half an hour in hand still. So what to do?

There should be plenty of time to intercept Mr. Pipewalla. And perhaps in that case it might bring the situation more under control, enable him to see some sort of alibi was put together for the fellow, if he were to make sure that the body was discovered reasonably soon.

Ring and report the murder anonymously. That would go some way, too, to satisfying his police officer's conscience.

Taking one last look around, he wrapped the bottom of one of Dolly Daruwala's pink silk curtains round the telephone receiver and, using his pen to dial, made the call.

Then he left, taking care not to close the outer door. Let the investigating officer who came make what he liked of that.

He decided to take the stairs again, even though it would be almost as toilsome as it had been to climb up. The last thing he wanted now was to be seen by any resident returning home who might later describe a man apparently leaving the scene of the crime. Slowly and thoughtfully he made his way down the poorly lit flights, the realm of the servants of the flats and such people as tailors or jewelry repairers summoned by the residents. The reek of urine was occasionally sharp in his nostrils.

It occurred to him shortly before he reached the bottom that it was more than likely that Burjor Pipewalla would in fact be waiting in his cousin's flat on the ground floor. What should he tell Mr. Mistry?

He halted for a moment at the dark turn of the next flight down and thought.

One thing was certain. He was not in any circumstances ever going to tell Mr. Mistry that Dr. Commissariat was Dolly Daruwala's killer. Even if Burjor Pipewalla was not waiting in his flat he would have to say that the murder had taken place. All too soon the news of that would be everywhere. But there was no reason why he should not say he had entered the flat and found Dolly Daruwala lying stabbed to death on the floor in front of her safe with all its contents fire-blackened. That was all Mr. Mistry, and Burjor Pipewalla, needed to know. They would be delighted to hear it, too.

Down at length at ground level, and happy in the thought that he had avoided being seen, he rang at Mr. Mistry's bell. After a little the door was opened, not by the servant with the terrible squint he had seen before but by Mr. Mistry himself.

"Inspector Ghote?" the Additional Secretary said in surprise, a tinge of anger already coming into his voice.

"Sir. Sir, it is most urgent. Is Mr. Burjor Pipewalla inside?"

"Well, yes, as a matter of fact, he is. But it is fifteen minutes at least before he is due to go up to that flat there. Why have you deserted your post? This is a serious matter, you know."

"Yes, sir. But something one hundred percent unexpected has occurred. May I come in, please?"

Mr. Mistry stood back and allowed Ghote to enter. As soon as the door was closed he gave the Additional Secretary the version of the circumstances he had contrived.

"Sir," he concluded, "I think it would be altogether best if Mr.

Pipewalla was immediately leaving this vicinity. My colleagues from the local station will be here in a very few minutes."

"Yes. Yes, Inspector, you are right. You have handled all this well. I shall remember."

The Dolly Daruwala murder, as Ghote had foreseen when he was thinking what to say to Mr. Mistry, very rapidly became big news. But what he had not foreseen, his mind full as it had been of the terrible event he had witnessed, an ominous black boulder poised to tumble forward, was that the murder would also very soon come much closer home for him. Yet the death of a person suspected of being the blackmailer of a good many influential Bombay citizens was a matter that naturally was referred with all speed to Crime Branch.

So when he arrived for work next morning, still experiencing moments when he doubted that he had seen what he had seen, it was to find the whole place buzzing with the affair and its consequences.

Not the least of those was the question of to whom would it fall to be the officer charged with the parallel investigation to that of the local police station which Crime Branch customarily made in important cases of this sort.

Suddenly, and sickeningly, Ghote thought: Will it be me?

But that fear at least was soon ended. Inspector Arjun Singh was allocated to the case.

For a few moments after he had heard this, Ghote was prey to sharp anxiety. Would Singh, who was a real hunter in his pursuit of criminals and would never have thought of letting even as patently fine a man as Dr. Commissariat go free, somehow come to learn that he himself was involved? The very frequency with which, as fellow officers on the same team, they were likely to meet might, in some extraordinary way, provide that hunter with some tiny clue to snuffle up.

But reason soon prevailed. No, he must see to it that there was nothing in his manner that could possibly betray him. And at least he had been scrupulous in checking that he had not left the least trace of his presence in that flat. Nor had he been seen anywhere near it. Except by Mr. Z. R. Mistry, and he of all people could be relied on not to breathe a word about the man he had sent up to spy on Dolly Daruwala.

In time perhaps, he allowed himself to think, even that looming black boulder in his mind would become mist hidden into an almost-forgotten occurrence.

But he had reckoned without one side effect of Inspector Singh being put on the case.

Halfway through the morning he was sent for by the Assistant Commissioner. Could this be something to do with the last time he had received orders in the big cabin, when he had been told to see Mr. Z. R. Mistry about a matter the Assistant Commissioner knew nothing about and wished to know nothing about? Was he perhaps going to receive a commendation, informal and without details of course, passed on from the Additional Secretary?

But the summons proved to be nothing of the kind.

"Ghote," the Assistant Commissioner said, "you may have heard that I have had to put Inspector Singh on this Daruwala murder. Very tricky implications, vital that we learn who is the culprit ek dum. But that means a certain matter Singh was due to deal with must go to someone else."

"Yes, sir?"

"It's a blackmail business. It was because Singh has experience in those sort of cases that I've put him on the Daruwala murder. Blackmail behind that almost certainly, as you must have heard. But I dare say you'll be able to handle this affair well enough. Not a great deal to it."

"Yes, sir."

"It's to do with the damn scandal sheet *Gup Shup*. Know it?"

"Yes, sir," Ghote answered quickly, since like almost everybody in Bombay with a command of English he was at least acquainted with the nature of the magazine that dispensed tittle-tattle and gossip, whether purely invented or with a substratum of truth, about any of the city's prominent people who came to its notice.

But in the back of his mind, he had some other, more

immediate memory of *Gup Shup*. A moment later it came to him. He nearly blurted it out on the spot.

A cold chill spiked through him. What if he had actually said aloud, "Yes, sir, I was seeing one copy of *Gup Shup* last night in the flat of Miss Dolly Daruwala itself?"

No, it was not going to be so easy to put into oblivion that scene he had witnessed. All the more so if, as luck would have it, he was now about to handle another case in which blackmail was involved.

Dimly he listened to what the Assistant Commissioner was telling him. Apparently in the absence in America of the notorious proprietor of *Gup Shup*, one Firdaus Kersasp, known always as Freddy Kersasp—his personal column had a bite and vigor that made it compulsory reading for thousands of Bombayites—his office manager, left in charge, had chosen to tackle a blackmail target himself. He had proposed, as Freddy Kersasp was supposedly frequently to do, that for a considerable payment to a sister publication to *Gup Shup* called *Indians of Merit and Distinction*, an unashamed vanity volume frequently promised and never as yet appearing, the magazine would not print an item hurtful to a certain Falli Bamboat, the young heir to a successful Parsi catering business who had achieved a considerable reputation as a Western classical pianist.

However Falli Bamboat had proved not to be as soft a target as the office manager, a Punjabi by the name of Shiv Chand, had counted on. He had actually come to the Assistant Commissioner and complained, and had gone as far as to nerve himself up to appear in court under the name of Shri X. This, it seemed, was the opportunity, long awaited, to put a check to *Gup Shup* and the irritation it had been causing to people who felt they should be free of any such annoyance.

So at least Ghote gathered from the Assistant Commissioner's somewhat guarded utterances. But to achieve this laudable aim, the Assistant Commissioner went on to point out, it would be necessary to obtain better evidence than the unsupported testimony of Shri X, Falli Bamboat. Once before an attempt had been made to convict Freddy Kersasp himself of blackmail, but thanks to a battery of high-powered pleaders, it had miserably failed.

"This time, Ghote, there will not be any mistake."

"No, sir."

The proposed handover of the sum that Shiv Chand had told Falli Bamboat would secure him an entry in *Indians of Merit and Distinction* in place of a nasty little item in *Gup Shup* was to be made next day. It would take place in the washroom at the Taj Mahal Hotel, believed to be the venue for more than one of Freddy Kersasp's own better-planned extortions. Ghote was to conceal himself there and witness the whole transaction.

But that of course was not all, as Ghote realized as soon as he had left the Assistant Commissioner's cabin. It would not be enough that a solitary police officer should overhear the blackmail attempt. They were not dealing here with anyone as ignorant of the ways of the legal world as Dolly Daruwala, who could have in all probability been scared out of the country on one police officer's word. Here it would be highly paid lawyers they would ultimately have to face. Everything must be done strictly according to the rules of the Criminal Procedure Code. And that meant that, not only would he himself have to witness the blackmail transaction, but that two independent witnesses, two panches, would have to be there in the washroom at the Taj Mahal Hotel as well.

No, it was not going to be as simple as the Assistant Commissioner had indicated.

At intervals all that day, as he dealt with the paperwork of other cases, he found himself worrying about the intricacies that would face him next day. He had, as soon as he had got back from the Assistant Commissioner, arranged with the nearby Lokmanya Tilak Road police station to have two panches, as respectable in appearance as they could find, ready for him to take to the Taj early next afternoon. Then he had got in touch with the securitywalla at the Taj and put him in the picture. But that was all he could think of to do by way of preparation.

All should be well, he kept telling himself.

And then he would remember with a sudden chill how he had

thought that all ought to have been well in what he had been asked to do in Dolly Daruwala's flat. And how badly that had gone wrong. The black boulder in his mind seemed then to lurch forward a fearful foot or two, however much he had striven to force it into the distance.

Eventually, however, his day came to an end and he made his way home. At least, he told himself, he should have a pleasant evening. Young Ved had been a little sulky ever since he had been rebuked over his smuggled home computer plan. But he had seemed gradually to be getting over it, and Protima had promised a particularly nice meal.

So it was with a doubly descending lurch of dismay that, when he had tapped for entrance, he saw on Protima's face as she opened the door a look of plain apprehension.

"Husbandji," she blurted out at once. "There is a man."

"A man? What man?"

"There. There. Look."

He turned in the direction she had indicated. And there, standing a discreet distance away, was a man he seemed to know but could not at first put a name to.

Then he realized who it was, if only from the fearful squint that disfigured the fellow's face. It was Mr. Z. R. Mistry's servant.

But what could he want? Had he been sent with a confidential letter? Something in writing to back up that swift word of praise last night? But, no, he had nothing in his hand. Was there some message, then? Was Mr. Mistry going to ask him to come and get that unpleasant cousin of his out of some new trouble?

Now the fellow was coming sidling up, reminding him of nothing so much as a scuttling, sharp-clawed crab. Behind, Protima pushed the door shut.

"It is Inspector Ghote."

He remembered then with a spurt of inner fury his mistake in announcing his rank as well as his name to this fellow when he had first called on Mr. Mistry.

"Yes. Yes, what it is you are wanting?"

He found he had spoken more spikily than the situation

seemed to warrant. But there was something in the fellow's manner that had made him suddenly wary.

"Name?" he demanded, sharply as before.

"It is Ranchod, Inspector sahib. Ranchod."

"Well, Ranchod, what are you wanting?"

"Only to show I am a friend, Inspector sahib."

"Friend? What friend? I am not needing you as any friend."

"Oh, Inspector sahib, I am thinking you are very much needing friend. Inspector, I was seeing you last night."

FIVE

Ghote knew at once what Mr. Mistry's squinting servant meant by saying that he had seen him the night before. The fellow must have caught sight of him just after he had left Dolly Daruwala's flat. He must believe that he himself was the murderer.

It was perfectly possible that in the darkness of the stairs at Marzban Apartments the fellow had been lying there in a corner of one of the landings near the top. Hurrying down, he himself could easily have altogether missed him. Yes, no doubt Mr. Mistry, expecting to entertain Burjor Pipewalla before that planned confrontation with the most dangerous woman in Bombay, had taken the precaution of giving his servant leave. The fellow, having nothing better to do, must have taken himself off to somewhere he knew was quiet and settled down to sleep.

He might then have had no more than a glimpse of this man he knew going quickly past on his way down. Only later would he have realized, with the arrival at the murder scene of the local police, what it must have been that this inspector whose name he had learned was apparently hurrying away from.

That squint-eyed face had so telegraphed menace that there could be no doubt about what the fellow had meant. But a

42

moment later at least the notion that he believed he himself was responsible for the murder was dispelled.

"Inspectorji, if you are wanting to help that man who was killing Daruwala memsahib, then that is okay by me."

No, this was worse. Ranchod must first have been wakened by Dr. Commissariat as he had departed by way of the stairs. Would he have recognized him? Had he perhaps been standing one evening in the doorway while Mr. Mistry was watching television, in the way that servants often did, and had seen on the news that same often-repeated shot of the famed Parsi scientist arriving in Bombay from America?

Again, however, his blackest fears proved unfounded.

Ranchod plastered an ingratiating half smile onto his face.

"But I am thinking it is altogether unfair if I am not sharing with you," he said.

"Sharing? What sharing?"

For a moment Ghote genuinely did not understand what the leering fellow was saying. But then he realized. The damn swine believed he, a police officer, was actually blackmailing Dolly Daruwala's murderer—thank God, he could not after all have seen enough of Dr. Commissariat as he had clattered past to know who he was—and he was brazenly asking for a cut.

He very nearly gave the fellow a slap that would have sent him sprawling.

But sense intervened.

After all, the impudent jackal must be certain that he himself had been in the flat at the time of the murder. If he was made an enemy of, it would be the easiest thing in the world for him to inform the local police station that a certain inspector knew the name of Dolly Daruwala's murderer and was choosing to keep his knowledge to himself. And there was never much love lost between station officers and Crime Branch men. Someone would get a lot of pleasure, and a lot of kudos, out of passing on to Vigilance Branch such a juicy piece of information.

"Well," he said cautiously, "perhaps we can talk."

Ranchod's squinting face broke into a lopsided grin, revealing a row of brown-stained stubs of teeth.

"Nothing to talk, bhai," he said. "Rupees one hundred needed only."

Inwardly Ghote boiled. How he would like to teach this badmash not to call him "brother." But at the same time, a cooler voice within considered the actual amount the fellow had mentioned.

It was not a very great deal. He could even produce it, though it would hurt a bit, simply by going inside and taking out the money they kept in a safe place for emergencies. Had it been only himself in question, he would, he was sure, have nevertheless acted on that famous Duke Wellington advice. Damn it, he had said to Ved it was the only answer to give to a blackmailer.

But it was not himself only he had to consider. It was Dr. Commissariat as well. The entire safety of that good and noble man was at stake. Refuse Ranchod that hundred rupees and he would almost certainly go around at once to his nearby police station, if only out of revengefulness. From there the matter would be passed rapidly on to Vigilance Branch. But it would not end simply with one Crime Branch officer being thrown out of the police. Any investigation was bound to be carried on to the point where the name of Dolly Daruwala's actual murderer came to light. Then Dr. Commissariat himself would be arrested and brought before the courts like a common criminal. It was unthinkable.

No, if handing over a hundred rupees would protect the brilliant scientist who had actually given up the prospect of great wealth to come to the aid of his poorer brothers, the sacrifice would surely be worth making.

Yet would a hundred rupees be all he would eventually have to hand over? Did he not have, still clanging in his mind, an example of how every blackmailer was tempted to operate? Dolly Daruwala and her repeated and repeated demands on Burjor Pipewalla. For that matter, he had heard Dr. Commissariat himself tell Dolly Daruwala he well realized that the one payment she was demanding was hardly likely to be the last.

But what else could he do now?

"All right," he said to the squinting fellow greedily regarding him still. "I will get your rupees one hundred. But let me tell you this: If ever you come anywhere near me again, I will see that you damn well regret it."

Next day, as he made efforts to get on with what routine work he had on his desk before the time came to go to the Taj Mahal Hotel and tackle the *Gup Shup* blackmailer, the scene with the squinting Ranchod came back time and again to Ghote's mind like bursts of sound issuing from a switched-off radio.

Should he really have let the fellow get away with his demand? What would Duke Wellington have done faced with his dilemma over Dr. Commissariat? Would he have still said publish and be damned? And what would Dr. Commissariat have done? Would he have been as active for good as he had been in dispatching Dolly Daruwala?

Well, one thing was clear, he thought. He himself could not eliminate his pest in the way the Parsi scientist had eliminated Dolly Daruwala. Not just for the sake of a hundred rupees. Not even to make sure of not being faced with a succession of demands for that sum. Not, surely, in fact for any reason.

Just after eleven o'clock a constable from Lokmanya Tilak Road police station brought around the two panches he was going to need that afternoon to witness with him the scene in the gentlemen's washroom of the Taj Mahal Hotel. At first sight he was distinctly pleased with whom he had been sent. He had gone to great lengths the day before on the telephone to impress upon the Lokmanya Tilak station house officer that he needed panches who were decent enough to be taken through the splendors of the Taj Mahal Hotel without attracting notice, and these two looked really respectable. They were a junior municipal building inspector, a young man with wide, frightened eyes and a narrow moustache, nervously twisting and twisting his hands together, and an aged Parsi, so thin that he looked like nothing so much as a long bag of rattling bones, dressed with scrupulous care in the white garments often clung to by the older members of his community. There would be no difficulty marching either of these two through the hotel into its washroom. In court eventually, too, they ought to make just the right impression.

But then a flicker of doubt about the Parsi came into his head. Would he, when it came to giving evidence, attempt to say too much because a fellow Parsi was the blackmailer's victim? And the old fellow's face seemed somehow familiar, too.

"Have I been seeing you somewhere before?" he asked him sharply.

The old man produced a shy grin.

"Oh, yes, Inspector," he answered. "Almost certainly."

"Where is that?" he demanded, his prickle of suspicion growing.

The old man's grin broadened a little.

"On television, Inspector," he replied. "I am the old Parsi in that advert they are showing and showing. Since I was retiring from my job at Anklesaria Sandalwood Mart I have joined film line. In my small way."

"Oh, yes. Yes, of course."

He could see the old man exactly now, smiling benevolently as he praised whatever it was that he was advertising. Though just what that was he could not for the life of him remember.

He glanced down at the chit the constable had brought, looking for his name.

"Listen, Mr. Framrose," he said eventually, "I am a little worried about making use of you. I do not think it would at all matter if His Honor in court is recognizing you from the TV. But in the case where we are requiring your services as a panch a Parsi also is very much involved. Now, what is going to happen when you are giving evidence about his each and every action?"

The old man straightened up a little.

"Inspector," he said, "I have always been accustomed to do my duty. And I well know what is the duty of a panch. It is to witness what occurs and to state the same in court, yes?"

"Certainly."

"Then that is what I will do, Inspector. I will faithfully tell what I have seen. That and no more."

* * *

So it was with fewer forebodings than he might have had that Ghote set off in good time for the Taj. And, there, everything seemed to go on going well. The security officer greeted the three of them, as arranged, at the staff entrance. He guided them rapidly through the magnificent foyer with its scatter of Indian and foreign guests dotted here and there on the richly covered sofas and its long, glintingly polished reception counter with its three or four receptionists in their elegant uniform saris. In less than two minutes they arrived at the heavy studded wooden door of the washroom.

Shiv Chand, the securitywalla murmured confidentially, had bribed the attendant on duty to make himself scarce for a quarter of an hour. So he, once he had extracted that information from the fellow, had allowed him to do as he had been asked.

"So, all yours, Inspector," he said. "And best of luck only."

"Thank you," Ghote replied, not altogether pleased that it should be thought necessary he should have the best of luck, or any luck at all.

But the thought of what had gone so terribly wrong during the last blackmailing attempt he had witnessed had entered his head once more, and he felt ominously that he well might need any luck that was going.

Leadenly he inspected the washroom's sparkling white marble walls, its deep basins, its row of heavy doors guarding the cubicles, and decided that the best he could do to conceal his two panches was to put them both behind the half-open door of the farthest cubicle. He showed them exactly where to stand and warned them of the need to be absolutely silent.

At once the first of his difficulties manifested itself. The young municipal building inspector seemed suddenly overcome by the splendor of his surroundings.

"Inspector sahib," he said, clasping and unclasping his hands with each time a sweaty little pop, "I am not at all liking it here."

"It is not a question of like or not like," Ghote said, unable to prevent himself snapping. "You are under orders. A person is not able to refuse when requested to act in the capacity of panch."

"But—but, Inspector, I am feeling sick only. Inspector, there is one heavy sweet odor in this place."

"Of course there is odor, you owl. It is some first-class disinfectant."

"But it is causing me very much of sickness."

Ghote felt his rage growing. At this rate he would be found arguing with the young man when Shiv Chand himself arrived.

"Take one drink of water only," he said to him sharply, indicating the gleamingly polished taps of the washbasins. "That will finish your all troubles."

The young man at least did as he had been told. Bending down to one of the taps, he noisily sucked in the flow of water.

Ghote turned to Mr. Framrose.

"And you," he asked, "are you feeling in any way sick?"

"Oh, no, Inspector. Long ago I was making up my mind that wherever you are in the world it is much the same. I have not had any opportunity till now to find myself in the place of the rich, but some nights in my room I put myself on the floor to sleep. I feel if the poor and the downtrodden can do it I should do it, too."

But Ghote had no time to think about that, or ask himself if he, too, should attempt such an exercise. The building inspector had risen from his crouching position over the spurting tap and was wiping his wet face with his hands.

"Now get back into place," he ordered him briskly. "And stay there, and do not make one single noise."

Meekly the young man obeyed.

Ghote hurried over and turned off the still gushing tap. He would have liked to have restored the basin to its previously gleaming state. But he suspected there was not time. Quickly he slipped into the cubicle next to the one occupied by his panches. He adjusted its door till he had a good view of the major part of the washroom through the crack at its hinges. Then he waited.

But he did not have to stand in his confined position long.

Hardly a minute had gone by when the door to the place was pushed cautiously and wheezingly open and a young man entered holding a cloth bag that might have contained a student's books. Although he was wearing the more or less anonymous shirt and trousers of all the Bombay middle class, Ghote had no difficulty in guessing he must be the Parsi, Falli Bamboat. He had the pale complexion of his community and, though young— little older than the wretched junior building inspector in the next cubicle, and almost as insecure-looking—early hair loss, again typical of an interbred Parsi, had made him three parts bald.

Altogether, he was not an impressive person. Would he ever be capable of playing the part he had agreed on in this encounter with the blackmailing Shiv Chand?

He wondered whether he might step out of his hiding place and offer the young man, who after all was being not uncourageous even in coming to the rendezvous, a word of encouragement. But, just in time, he heard the door wheeze open again, this time pushed with vigorous determination.

Shiv Chand—from the rapid and purposeful survey he immediately made, if from nothing else, could only be the blackmailer—was a burly individual of about fifty. His face was large, broad of jaw, prominent of nose, with somewhat scanty graying hair well-oiled and brushed hard back. His mouth wore a wide shark's grin.

Ghote held his breath and locked his every muscle. Fervently he hoped the two in the next cubicle were keeping equally silent.

The *Gup Shup* office manager took a step or two farther in, ignoring Falli Bamboat, who seemed paralyzed already into total silence. Then he stood still and looked all around. Ghote, holding his breath until he felt near to bursting, tried to send thought waves of warning to his two panches.

Shiv Chand took another step forward. It was plain he was making for the first of the row of cubicles with the aim of checking that he and Falli Bamboat were alone.

Ghote, beads of sweat emerging on face and neck, foresaw his whole plan cascading into ruin. If the big Punjabi was going to say not a word until, one by one, he had looked into each of the cubicles, discovery would be certain. But where else could he have hidden himself? Where else put his encumbering panches?

Then, with the suddenness of a rock fall rattling from an ages-locked mountainside, Falli Bamboat spoke.

"It is Mr. Shiv Chand? I am Mr. Falli Bamboat. Have I come at the right time? This was the hour you were mentioning, yes? I was worried that I might be too late. Or too early even. But I did not relish staying in here with no reason, if I had come too soon."

Well done. Oh, well done. Shabash, young man. Shabash.

Ghote, realizing what the young Parsi pianist was doing to halt Shiv Chand's search, almost spoke the words aloud.

"Ah," Shiv Chand said pouncingly at last. "Mr. Bamboat. Good afternoon."

Falli Bamboat did not in answer begin well.

"Good—good—good morning. No, good afternoon."

"Well, Mr. Bamboat, it is a very good afternoon for you, I am thinking. To have your name and fame only in *Indians of Merit and Distinction* and at a so-early age, that is something altogether great, yes?"

Ghote, his cheek pressed hard against the crack of his cubicle door, saw Falli Bamboat jerk back his shoulders in a visible effort to regain some initiative.

"Yes," he said at last. "Yes, that is all very well. But if I am to pay the large amount you were mentioning on the telephone for that privilege, can I be perfectly sure that a certain item will not appear in—"

He came to an abrupt halt as if it was hardly possible for him to pronounce the name of the gossip magazine in which an account of his guilty secret, whatever it was, was threatened.

Then with a strangulated cough he managed to continue.

"In, that is, in *Gup Shup*."

Well done again, young man, Ghote thought. You are driving him to state his business in words that we can witness. Shabash, shabash.

"My dear sir," Shiv Chand answered. "You have only to ask and that little item will be cast in the dustbin straightaway. You know, we are not at all liking to print anything that is causing offense. Not at all, not at all."

"I have only to ask?" Falli Bamboat inquired pointedly.

In one of the heavy mirrors above the row of basins Ghote was able to see the Punjabi's shark smile widen yet farther.

"Well, no beating about the bushes," he said. "You cannot ask such a favor until you are our friend only. Until you have become a valued entrant in *Indians of Merit and Distinction*. Until you have made one payment for your insertion."

"And that payment is to be ten thousand rupees?"

Mentally Ghote applauded him yet again. The young man was by no means as timid as he looked. This was exactly what the two hidden panches ought to hear, and ought in due time to tell a court that they had heard.

"Yes, yes," Shiv Chand said amiably. "That was indeed the sum we mentioned telephonically."

Falli Bamboat managed a convincing gulp.

"Very well," he said. "Here's your money."

He reached into his cloth bag and took from it not books but thick bundles of currency notes. He held them out in a heaped mess between both his hands.

With a new smile of sharklike pleasure Shiv Chand leaned forward and gathered them up.

Ghote took one long step out of his hiding place.

"Mr. Shiv Chand," he said, "I am a police officer, and I am arresting you under Section Three-eight-three of the Indian Penal Code, intentionally putting a person in fear and thereby dishonestly inducing them to deliver any valuable security, thus committing extortion."

SIX

Ghote hardly dared to believe that the arrest of Shiv Chand had gone so smoothly. And before long he found that he was right to have felt twinges of doubt. The Assistant Commissioner congratulated him, briefly, on the success. Then he added something more.

"But, of course, Chand isn't the fellow they really want."

A dart of alarm went through Ghote at that word *they*. He did not know who exactly the Assistant Commissioner was referring to, and he certainly had no intention of asking. But he realized altogether too clearly that someone up above, probably high, high up above, must have insisted at some time recently that something should be done about the activities of *Gup Shup*. Probably a friend of a friend of a friend had been one of the magazine's victims and his objections had been passed on.

And, he thought with rapidly increasing dismay, it was clear now that none other than himself was to be put in charge of doing whatever was to be done.

Once more he cursed the Dolly Daruwala business. If Dolly Daruwala had not been killed, then this new task, with all its threatened complications, would no doubt have fallen to thrustful Inspector Arjun Singh, expert on blackmail.

But no use in wishing and wanting.

"It is Mr. Freddy Kersasp himself we must be placing behind the bars?" he asked, well knowing the answer.

"It is, Inspector, and I am looking to you to do it."

"Yes, sir."

"Right, go and put that Shiv Chand of yours through the damn mill. Get him to tell you all about Mr. Kersasp. And don't be too pussyfoot in the way you go about it. I want results, Ghote. Results."

So an evening that he had thought he would spend at home was devoted instead to a face-to-face confrontation with Shiv Chand. The evening, and the greater part of that night.

To no avail. The Punjabi stubbornly avoided telling him anything about his employer that was not already common knowledge.

Eventually Ghote even abandoned the pussyfooting the Assistant Commissioner had instructed him not to employ. But long before he did so he had caught on to what was making his prisoner so determined to give nothing away. Freddy Kersasp was still in America. Without some indication of his boss's attitude to the failure of his own attempt at blackmail, Shiv Chand was going to make sure he did not commit himself in any way.

However, realizing all that did not mean that Ghote did not feel obliged to go on trying to prise something out of the fellow. To go on and on. If next morning the Assistant Commissioner asked what results he had got, he did not like to think what the reaction would be if he answered that almost from the start he had come to the conclusion they would get nowhere till Freddy Kersasp was back in Bombay.

But at last it became obvious that even making the burly Punjabi stand in front of his desk for hour after hour without a break, without refreshment, without even a cigarette was not going to break him. So, with a bang on his bell to summon a constable to take the prisoner away and lock him up, he gave up.

But, he reflected, wearily making his way home through the deserted streets—deserted except for the dozens of pavement sleepers on this oppressively hot night—one fact at least he had squeezed out. Freddy Kersasp was not expected back at the *Gup Shup* offices for at least two weeks.

The next day began badly, even before Ghote had got to headquarters and the expected summons to let the Assistant Commissioner know what he had done about Shiv Chand. The trouble was young Ved.

Bleary still after his very short night, just as he was grabbing a hasty breakfast before setting off, Ved appeared at his side.

"Dadaji?"

"Yes? What is it? I am going in one or two minutes, you know."

"There is something I am wanting to ask."

"Yes?"

Ved stayed silent.

"Yes? Speak up, speak up. I have said I must go."

"Dadaji, it is that home computer."

At the very mention of the machine, anger flared up in him. He knew it was triggered not so much by the thought of the computer itself as by the revival of Ved's youthful attempt at blackmail and, looming up behind that once more, the black boulder of witnessing how Dolly Daruwala had met her end. But the knowledge did nothing to bring him calm.

He swung around from the remains of the crisply fried puris in front of him.

"Now, listen to me," he barked out at Ved. "I want to hear nothing more about that computer. Nothing ever again. Ever. Understood?"

"Yes, Dadaji."

Ved looked blankly crestfallen. But, though in the ordinary way the sight of him so distressed would at once have evaporated all anger, now it had no effect.

"I hope it is understood," he repeated. "Home computer is a banned subject in this house. From now on. Cent percent."

In front of the Assistant Commissioner, however, things went better than they might have done. He was, as he had known he would be, treated to a few harsh words about his failure immediately to have extracted from the *Gup Shup* office manager any damning evidence against its proprietor. But the Assistant Commissioner soon conceded that, with Freddy Kersasp in America, it was in fact not very practical to push the investigation any further for the time being.

"The damn fellow will be fully informed on the arrest of Shiv Chand by now," he concluded. "So perhaps, with one piece of good luck, he will take it into his head to stay on in America once and for all. Then one damn business at least will be off my hands."

"Yes, sir."

"In the meantime, Ghote, you have other work, yes?"

"Yes, sir. Always plenty."

"Good. Well, get on with it, then. Get on with it. And we will let your Shiv Chand stew in his own juices until it is clear whether Mr. Freddy Kersasp is or is not returning home."

When ten days later he learned from the *Gup Shup* offices that Freddy Kersasp had apparently postponed his return for at least an extra week, he began to hope the Assistant Commissioner had been right. Warned by the failure of his employee's piece of blackmailing, Freddy Kersasp was perhaps cutting his losses and establishing himself in the United States with whatever ill-gotten gains he had succeeded in smuggling out of India. Then, with luck, he would let *Gup Shup* close down, and whoever it was up there who had been made anxious could smile once more.

Somehow the relief Ghote felt extended in a mysterious fashion to his other, secret fear. He began to hope that Inspector Arjun Singh, whom he still continued to avoid, would never get on the trail of the murderer of Dolly Daruwala. Perhaps the black boulder that had seemed to loom topplingly in his mind was beginning already to be lost to sight.

When after another week he learned that Freddy Kersasp was prolonging his stay in America yet again, he went for hours without once seeing in his mind Dr. Commissariat standing over Dolly Daruwala's body and his gupti sword protruding from her rose-pink sari. Only when tiredness overtook him in the evening did that vision come swimming back again.

But his state of increasing content was not to run on indefinitely.

On the day that fell exactly one month after Dolly Daruwala's murder, he found, returning home in the evening, Ranchod once again waiting for him outside his door. The fellow was smiling ingratiatingly and squinting horribly. So, after all, he had realized that the possession of a secret gave a blackmailer more than one opportunity. Even if, from that forced smile of his, he had as yet acquired nothing of the iciness of Dolly Daruwala herself.

What was he to do about him?

He was plainly not yet in a position to send him about his business, if he ever was going to be. Arjun Singh might not have got any nearer knowing who had killed Dolly Daruwala, but Dr. Commissariat was by no means safe. Ranchod was still able, if his demands were not met, to start inquiries that were bound to lead eventually to the Parsi scientist.

Nothing for it, then, but at least to find out how much the fellow wanted.

"Well?" he barked out at him.

"Inspector sahib, good evening."

"You are wanting something, yes?"

The fellow smiled more wholeheartedly then, the brown stubs of his teeth apparent.

"Inspectorji, I am thinking you are well knowing what I am needing. Bad needing, Inspector."

Plainly another hundred rupees was going to be demanded, though why the fellow should feel he had to claim that his need was urgent was something of a mystery. After all, he was getting pay, boarding, and lodging from Mr. Mistry.

"All right. One hundred rupees. But for the last time."

"Oh, yes, yes, Inspector. Very-very last time only."

Luckily he had replaced their emergency cash within a couple of days of having paid Ranchod before. He tapped at his door and when Protima opened to him he told her he needed some money in a hurry. Without letting her see the hovering blackmailer, he went in, took the hundred rupees from its hiding place, and quickly stepping outside again, thrust the notes into Ranchod's expectant hand.

"The last time," he repeated ferociously.

Yet he suspected in fact this would hardly be Ranchod's final appearance.

Then, just two days later, making what he had come to regard as merely a routine call to the *Gup Shup* offices, he was told that Mr. Freddy Kersasp was back. He felt a dull shock of disappointment. True, he had not allowed himself fully to hope that the scandal magazine's proprietor would pass out of his life, and Bombay's, altogether. But he had bit by bit got used to the idea that finding evidence against him was something he would never have to do.

However, long beforehand he had worked out what his first step should be if the *Gup Shup* proprietor should return. He would at once inform him that he had no objection to his visiting his employee held on a blackmail charge.

Either then Freddy Kersasp would back Shiv Chand, or he would disown him. If he did the former, then it would be a matter of trying in every way to link the blackmail attempt, for which they had such satisfactory proof, back from Shiv Chand to Freddy Kersasp himself. If, as he guessed was more likely, Freddy Kersasp attempted to sever all links with his office manager, then, with any luck, the Punjabi would begin telling whatever he knew to Freddy Kersasp's discredit.

He got an inkling of what Freddy Kersasp's attitude would be when, telephoning to give him this message, he failed to get through.

"But I am wanting to speak with him concerning his employee, one Mr. Shiv Chand, now under arrest," he said.

And back came the answer.

"Mr. Shiv Chand is no longer an employee of *Gup Shup* Enterprise (Private) Limited. Mr. Kersasp's instruction."

He felt, on the whole, pleased.

Surely when he took that blank rejection to Shiv Chand the shark smile would be wiped from his face.

It was.

"Does he think he can be doing this to me also?" the burly Punjabi shouted. "I will be teaching him. My God, yes."

"Then you are knowing matters to Mr. Kersasp's discredit?"

"Matters I am knowing. One hundred, two hundred."

"Well then, Mr. Chand, let us get down to details," Ghote said, sliding at once into a much more friendly tone than in his previous dealings with the office manager.

Between them in the course of the next two hours they produced, not two hundred or even one hundred, but four recent clear instances, which Shiv Chand clamored to vouch for if he was permitted to turn Approver, of blackmail attempts Freddy Kersasp had conducted in person. Each one, Shiv Chand said quoting figures, would have netted a substantial sum for promised biographies in that ever-unprinted volume, *Indians of Merit and Distinction*.

With feelings of considerable satisfaction Ghote took his findings to the Assistant Commissioner.

"No good, Inspector."

"Sir, no good? But—"

"Inspector, we are not dealing with some two-per-paisa hanky-panky fellow snatching a fruit from some handcartwalla. We are dealing with a man who once before has been up in court and has walked out from it. What we are needing are evidences that God Krishna himself could not laugh off."

"Yes, sir. But what—"

"Inspector, take each and every one of these cases your Shiv Chand has given you, get to the people involved, and come away with their assurances, hard and fast, that they will come into court, Shri X, Shri Y, or Shri ABC, and back up what your fellow is saying. Do that, Inspector, and we would be in business."

"Yes, sir."

As Ghote turned to go, there rose up in his mind, more vivid than ever before, that vision again of Dolly Daruwala lying dead in front of her safe full of secrets. If, he said to himself with bitterness, that vermin, snake, or pest had not been eliminated, however justly, it would be Inspector Arjun Singh and not Inspector Ghote who would be looking at one gloomy future.

SEVEN

In the days that followed, Ghote's forebodings about his immediate future proved pleasantly accurate. None of the four people the Assistant Commissioner had ordered him to persuade into being Mr. X, Mr. Y, Mr. Z, or Mr. ABC were at all willing even to see him.

It took three days of repeated telephone calls, speaking to evasive secretaries, obstructive clerks, unhelpful servants, before he succeeded in securing an appointment with one of them. This was a Mr. Suresh Jesingbhai, a Gujarati stockbroker. According to Shiv Chand, Mr. Jesingbhai had paid heavily for his inclusion, at some vague future date, in *Indians of Merit and Distinction* rather than have it put before the world in *Gup Shup*, implacably appearing every two weeks, that he had once had a certain arrangement with a telephone operator. In the days before the Bombay telephone system had become automated, this lady had not only put through any urgent dealings for him at lightning-call speed, but had also seen that someone else's bill was debited. Then, after the good times were over, she had eventually realized that she could make further extra income by selling the story to Freddy Kersasp.

When Ghote had at last got through to Mr. Jesingbhai in person and had discreetly hinted at the nature of his business, he had been given a reluctant appointment. It was for late in the evening at Mr. Jesingbhai's office.

Tapping at the outer door, the dimmest of lights only behind its glass panel inscribed JESINGBHAI AND CO. in aged flaking black paint, Ghote thought what an unimpressive place it was that he had come to. But from his careful preliminary inquiries it was clear that, dingy though the office seemed, vast sums were made in it. The world of the Dalal Street brokers was notorious for the size of its wealth behind often the shabbiest of exteriors.

Mr. Jesingbhai, who came himself to draw back the several bolts on the door, fully lived up to that image. He was dressed in the traditional Gujarati mode, a white kurta with a thickly pleated dhoti hanging down from his ample stomach and a heavily sweat-stained black cap on his head. It was difficult in the poor light to see much of his face, but Ghote received a distinct impression of sullen suspiciousness emanating from thickly podgy features.

After responding to a grunted demand for identification, he was at last admitted. Following the bulky white shape of the broker, he was aware in the ineffectual light coming from a single low-powered bulb of clerks' desks topped with cracked plastic, of folding chairs with thin rexine-covered seats, of a tiled floor pitted and uneven. A distinct smell of urine was seeping in from somewhere, and although he saw an air conditioner, it was hanging crazily from one of the small high windows plainly long awaiting repair.

At his own inner office Mr. Jesingbhai carefully closed the door and put his bulk firmly against it. Then he spoke.

"That girl is one filthy liar. She was telling what she did just only because I was refusing her money. Not one word is true."

Ghote, reflecting that here was an unlikely believer in Duke Wellington's advice to those threatened with blackmail, swallowed once.

"Mr. Jesingbhai," he said, "please understand, as I was stating per telephone there would be no question of any prosecution for any illegal actions you yourself may or may not have committed."

"Nothing I have done."

"Well, let us not argue about that. But it is our information from a one hundred percent reliable source that you were making a payment of rupees ten thousand to one Mr. Firdaus, or Freddy, Kersasp for bio-data to be inserted in the book *Indians of Merit and Distinction*."

"Proof. What proof are you having?"

"Sir, account entry itself," Ghote boldly lied, reasonably certain that Shiv Chand's information had been accurate.

In the better light from the single neon tube that hung over Mr. Jesingbhai's desk, he saw the broker shoot him a look of sharp distrust.

"No prosecution? You were stating there would be no prosecution? You would give me your word? Your word of honor? On paper?"

"Sir, I will write it here and now only."

Another darting look. But the broker did not appear to see the need to take him up on his offer.

"Very well, Inspector. But what it is exactly you are wanting? Of course, you are understanding I will aid and assist the police in every way within my powers."

"Thank you, sir. I know I can rely on you as an honest citizen to do your duty."

"Yes, yes. But what duty it is?"

Ghote wished he could have led around more carefully to the request he had to make. But Mr. Jesingbhai had put his question.

"Sir," he said, "Commissioner sahib himself is wishing that you, appearing just only under the name of Shri X, would give evidence against Mr. Kersasp on the charge of blackmail."

"Blackmail? Blackmail, Inspector? But it is not myself who has been blackmailed by Mr. Kersasp. It is that girl only who was attempting to blackmail me. If it is that one you are charge-sheeting evidence as Shri X, I would give and give. There is not going to be much of notice taken to one case like that."

"And you are fearing that notice would be taken of a case involving Mr. Freddy Kersasp?" Ghote said. "But, sir, I can assure you the greatest precautions would—"

"Precautions nothing, Inspector. Come, you and I are well

knowing that if that Mr. Kersasp is taken into court, entire
Bombay would be wanting to know what about it all was. And
would get to know also. Before you could be saying Chakravar-
tyrajagopalachari."

Too late for persuasion now, Ghote thought dismally. Only
thing is some tough talking.

"Mr. Jesingbhai," he said, "the fact of matter is that you have
paid rupees ten thousand to Mr. Kersasp. What is that if it is not
blackmail? You are knowing fully well something to your
discredit was threatened to be printed in *Gup Shup* magazine. It
is your bounden duty to give evidence when we are bringing the
culprit to court."

Mr. Jesingbhai gave him a look of sheer cunning.

"Inspector, evidence is it that I am paying for bio-data in that
Indians of Merit book? But paying for that is something I can do
if I am wanting, no?"

Ghote sighed.

"Sir, you and I are both well knowing that it is not at all truly
likely any person would pay so much for such a return only."

"But that is what I was paying. And for that only, Inspector."
The broker stared at him with blank hostility.

Above, he was conscious suddenly that the neon tube hanging
there was giving out a thin little buzz. And he knew he had come
to the end of this road.

There were, however, still three more roads to follow. And,
despite the Assistant Commissioner's order to secure Shri X, Shri
Y, Shri Z, and Shri ABC as witnesses, if in fact it turned out that
just one of the four was prepared eventually to give evidence
against Freddy Kersasp, they could then safely bring their case.
But nevertheless he felt cold depression sliding over him.

As soon as he had sat himself at his desk the following day he
rang, yet again, the next most likely *Gup Shup* victim on his list.
This was a very different sort of businessman from the tradition-
alist Gujarati Mr. Jesingbhai. Ramesh Deswani was, he had
learned from Shiv Chand, a self-made success, a pushful Sindhi,
managing director of Despruf Waterproofing, selling a much-

vaunted system for keeping monsoon rains from penetrating Bombay's thousands of flat-roofed buildings. Shiv Chand, taking a quick look once at Freddy Kersasp's well-hidden "true" account books, as opposed to those made up for the income tax authorities, had seen the *Indians of Merit and Distinction* entry for Ramesh Deswani's payment of no less than twenty thousand rupees. Shiv Chand had not, however, managed to worm out of his employer before he had left for America just what it was that *Gup Shup* would have printed if Ramesh Deswani had declined to accept the honor offered him.

The call to Despruf Waterproofing's offices brought at least some luck. He did not, of course, succeed in speaking to Ramesh Deswani himself. But, talking with his secretary, he heard a voice in the background shouting in English, with a touch of hysteria, he thought, "No, not today. Tomorrow. Perhaps tomorrow."

He began to hope that he had found a possibly willing witness. First thing next day he would be on the telephone again.

In the meanwhile he conscientiously tried at regular intervals the other two names on his list, a retired Major-General Kalgutkar, whose son had done something that would have made a nice item for the innuendo-filled pen of Freddy Kersasp, and a lady who had recently been made Bombay's Inspector of Smoke Nuisances, the first woman to hold the post. But he was not too dismayed when, first, the general's servant answered that his master was "not at home" and then a clerk told him that the Inspector of Smoke Nuisances was "unavailable." He still had the managing director of Despruf Waterproofing in his sights, and plenty of routine work to be getting on with.

Next morning he got an utterly unexpected hint as to what the trouble might have been that had put Ramesh Deswani into Freddy Kersasp's power. Thinking when he had arrived in his office that it was really too early to make the call he hoped would now be accepted, he decided to take a few minutes to look at the *Indian Post*. And there the first thing that caught his eye was news about his potential witness.

"Bombay Firm Chief Leaps to His Death," a headline read. Then followed:

New Delhi, Apl 21 (UNI). The body of Ramesh Deswani, 56, managing director of Despruf Ltd., Bombay, was discovered on the service floor of a newly constructed four-star hotel on Asoka Road here last night. The police said Deswani, who arrived here earlier yesterday, had checked in at the hotel and was lodged in room 703 on the seventh floor. His shoes were found on the sixteenth floor. The police said a suicide note was also discovered, which said: "I have committed serious mistakes and I feel I should destroy myself." It was written in English.

He sat there, staring at the page, seeing nothing.

At once it had come into his mind that it was none other than he himself who was responsible for Ramesh Deswani's death. It must surely have been the repeated calls from someone announcing himself as an inspector of police that had made this pushful, successful businessman believe whatever secret he had had that he had paid Freddy Kersasp not to mention in *Gup Shup* had somehow become known. In all probability it was not, in fact, the police Ramesh Deswani had to fear so much as the income tax authorities. But no doubt, with it made clear to him through Freddy Kersasp how vulnerable his secret was, the weight on his conscience had become too heavy. So he had abruptly taken flight to distant Delhi and there in the loneliness of a hotel room he had made up his mind to end his life.

But no, he thought. Damn it, he was not to blame for that death. Freddy Kersasp was. Making those twenty thousand rupees from finding out about Ramesh Deswani's "serious mistakes"—however that secret had been learned—was what had begun the slide that had ended in a jump to death from the sixteenth floor of a four-star hotel in Delhi. This was what Freddy Kersasp's cheerful gossip sheet could bring about. And no doubt others over the years had paid a similar price for declining to hide the past under a long, and costly, entry in *Indians of Merit and Distinction*.

Back into his mind, more blackly than ever, came the vision now of Dolly Daruwala's safe with its fat store of dangerous documents just before Dr. Commissariat had set light to them, and of Dolly Daruwala herself in her rose-pink sari lying dead at its foot.

Furiously he flapped the pages of the *Indian Post* together and stuffed them down on the floor beside his desk. He picked up the telephone.

Come what may, he would find one witness with courage enough to go into court and testify against a blackmailer.

But mere determination was not sufficient. Neither of the remaining two people Shiv Chand had pointed him to would even accept his calls.

"He would be ringing back."

"She will ring back."

How often he had heard such replies in the past few days. And not once had his telephone shrilled out.

It was not, in fact, until two days later that he contrived to contact one of the two, Major-General Kalgutkar. He, according to Shiv Chand, had gained his place in *Indians of Merit and Distinction* not of course for his distinguished army career, though that had been notably distinguished. Instead it was his son, also in the army, Captain Kalgutgar, who had been so indiscreet as to give Freddy Kersasp his lever. Captain Kalgutkar had taken to leading a band of young officers with nothing better to do careering around the countryside near Poona spotting girls in love trysts they would do anything to keep their parents from learning about. He had then forced the girls to take part in making blue films. Somehow these activities had come to the notice of Freddy Kersasp, known always to be on the lookout for such juicy items, and a request to the captain's father had followed.

Trying the general's number for the fifteenth or sixteenth time, Ghote was lucky to find it answered by the man himself. Quickly darting in, he told him what it was he wanted to discuss.

"Good God, I can't speak about something like that on the phone."

"No, sir. I am altogether understanding. Would you like to make appointment to talk here at Crawford Market Headquarters?"

"And what do you think my friends would say seeing me marching in there?"

Privately Ghote thought they would assume he had some minor business to conduct. But, feeling himself a monkey-catcher about to lure a timid jungle creature into his bamboo cage, he asked instead where the general would like to meet him. After a good deal of humming and hawing—"No, damn it. Promised the memsahib to go to some charity function that evening"—the general fixed on the Hanging Gardens shortly before they closed for the night. Three days ahead.

Ghote felt a ripple of anger.

Why was he making so much of a fuss? Army life must have made him security mad only.

All too clearly he saw during the three waiting days this one but last hope of his getting cold feet. Yet there was nothing he could do other than agree to both time and place.

In the intervening days, however, he did not cease trying to secure a similar meeting with the final name on his list, the lady who had recently been appointed, to some press comment, as Inspector of Smoke Nuisances, a Mrs. Amrita Nath. But he found, as he had found before, the clerks in her office possessed a sixth sense about calls she would not want to receive. Nor in two more long sessions with Shiv Chand did he manage to find any other potential witnesses about whom there were good hard facts.

So it was with more than a little anxiety that he took himself on the evening Major-General Kalgutkar had specified up Malabar Hill to the Hanging Gardens, built over the huge water tanks that fed the teeming city below. The general had suggested as a rendezvous point the children's playground, no doubt deserted at the late hour he had chosen.

"I trust you are not going to appear in anything other than mufti, Inspector," he had snapped.

"No, sir. Of course not, sir. Crime Branch officers are wearing uniform on special occasions only."

"Very well. So you had better carry some identification. Bring a packet of cigarettes. Chancellor brand. Kind I smoke myself."

Feeling not a little foolish, Ghote approached the playground, holding in front of himself conspicuously as he could the packet of Chancellors he had had considerable difficulty in getting hold of. None of the paanwallas he had tried had stocked them, and one had even assured him the brand no longer existed. Eventually he had found them at the Woodlands Restaurant in the towers-crammed Nariman Point business area. But when the waiter told him the packet of twenty cost eighteen rupees, he had looked so shocked—five or six days' supply, he had at once thought, would be as much as squint-eyed Ranchod was demanding as his monthly blackmail—that the waiter had suggested "One stick itself is ek rupee only, sir." And then he had had some difficulty in insisting on having a whole packet after all.

He looked about for anyone who might be the general.

In a minute he spotted a tall trim figure in an open-necked khaki bush-shirt, wearing a white flat cap, and with a neat white moustache in the middle of a sharply authoritative face. He tilted the cigarette packet till its front was clearly visible. But the general—if it was the general—did not respond.

Another dead end. Where was the damn man? Had he decided after all not to come?

All his troubles came rushing back into his mind and in a spat of fury he crushed the wretched pack of Chancellors to a mashed-up squab.

Could the general then be one of the group of men who had taken over a corner of the children's playground as a sort of gym? They were using the slides and swings as exercise-bars, solemnly heaving themselves up and down. Was the general so afraid of being seen talking to a police officer that he had adopted such an extraordinary subterfuge? Surely not.

He looked round once more. High up against the paling sky

there still circled a few vultures, always to be seen in the vicinity
of the nearby Towers of Silence, where the Parsis laid out their
dead so as not to defile earth, fire, or water. The sight put into his
head once again the memory, as little to be got rid of as a fruit
seed lodged in the teeth, of dead Dolly Daruwala. Had her
funeral ceremonies taken place at the Towers, despite the way she
had scorned all the traditions of her community, despite the evil
path her life had taken? Or had her body been disposed of
without ceremony or mourners?

A Parsi boy, years ago at college, had told him once that the
souls of the dead visit their homes while the four days of
prescribed prayers are being said and a lamp filled with coconut
oil has to be kept burning in welcome at the head of their beds.
With no lamp lit for her, would Dolly Daruwala's icy soul forever
hover around the two people who had seen her die?

A voice spoke suddenly right in his ear. He jumped in surprise.

"Are those cigarettes you've got squashed up there Chancellor
brand?"

He wheeled around. It was the man with the white flat cap at
whom he had pointed the packet so meaningfully as soon as he
had arrived.

"It is Gener—"

"Quiet, man, no names."

He strove to suppress another spurt of amazed anger. Surely
coming all the way up here to meet was taking precautions
enough? Did the general think the safety of India itself was at
stake?

But he must be humored at all costs. This was his best hope of
securing a witness prepared to do his simple duty. An upright
soldier. A gentleman.

"It is most good of you to meet, sir."

"Well, I'll tell you straight out. I haven't come here by choice."

"No, sir, I am well understanding. It is altogether somewhat
embarrassing. But Commissioner sahib himself is one hundred
percent anxious to put an end to the proposed volume *Indians of
Merit and Distinction*. He is hoping for your full cooperation."

"Then we had better have some plain speaking right away. I am quite prepared to admit to you—in private, understand—that I would never have paid so much as one rupee to have my career described in that bloody book. But that shit Kersasp—only word for the fellow—came to me with a story he had got hold of about that son of mine. Disgraceful business, and I've told the boy so in no uncertain terms. But I didn't like to think of the sordid details being spread all over that beastly scandal sheet for every member of the Cricket Club of India to see. So I paid up and put a good face on it."

"Yes, sir. I can well see it. But nevertheless . . . sir, isn't it that you have a duty? A duty to put a stop to the nefarious activities of such a person as Mr. Kersasp?"

The general shot him a glance that, even in the fading light, seemed to have in it a good deal more of anger than of suspicion.

"Don't you tell me anything about duty, Inspector," he barked.

Ghote noted that now abruptly the general had altogether abandoned the somewhat absurd security measures he had previously insisted on. He had not faltered for an instant when he had uttered the word *Inspector* loudly enough to have come to the ears of the playground gymnasts now ceasing their gyrations and moving over to the rail where they had hung their clothes.

Nevertheless he must not let himself be intimidated by this new, more forceful soldier surprisingly emerging.

"Sir," he said, "I have mentioned duty because it is one hundred percent definite that you are having a duty. Sir, it is the duty of every citizen of India to do what has to be done to bring to justice whosoever may be breaking the laws of our country."

Evidently his firmness had had some effect.

Again the general gave him a glare from under the white eyebrows that echoed his neat white moustache. But now there was in the glare—he was certain of it, dim though instant by instant the light was becoming—a quiver of hesitation. An acknowledged doubt.

"Yes, Inspector, there is that duty. You are right. You do well to speak of it, however much it's neglected and ignored up and down the country today."

The general glanced down momentarily at the ground at his feet.

In the air around them Ghote was conscious of the faint coolness of the coming night.

The general lifted his head.

"I would like to think, Inspector, that I was one of those, one of the few I venture to say, who recognized the duty you've spoken of and did what they were called on to do."

Again, for the space of half a second, his gaze dropped to the ground. Then he continued.

"But the fact of the matter is—damn it all, if it was only a matter of protecting a son of mine from the consequences of his own folly I wouldn't have hesitated to tell a filthy blackmailer like Kersasp, in the words of the famous Duke of Wellington, to publish and be damned. Heard of the Duke, Inspector?"

"Oh, yes, sir," Ghote answered, feeling a sharp stab.

"Ancestor of mine fought against him here in India, you know. Long before he tackled Napoleon and was made a duke."

The general gave an angry twitch to his neat moustache.

"That's the whole point really," he said. "Honor of the family. May seem a bit of a nonsense to you, Inspector. But means one hell of a lot to me. If that shit had printed all that about my boy in his beastly rag, we'd have had an inquiry. Bound to have done. And in the end the boy would have had to resign his commission. And he's the only one in the line, you see. Only one left. To carry on. Do what Kalgutkars have done since—since, damn it, time immemorial."

He came to yet another halt.

Ghote, looking at him with anxiety, guessing what was to come, thought he saw, despite the dusk, something in the general's sharp gray eyes that must be a glistening of tears.

"Sir—" he began, not quite knowing how he was going to finish.

But the general plunged on.

"Damn it, I know what my duty is. I ought to treat that fellow Kersasp as he deserves to be treated. Duty as a soldier. Duty, as you've rightly pointed out, as a citizen. But the truth of it is, I can't help feeling I've got a higher duty. Duty to tradition. And—and—"

He brought himself rigidly to attention as if he was facing a firing squad.

"It's no good, Inspector," he said, forcing the words out. "That's the duty I'm going to stick by. Come what may."

He let out a sound that was somewhere between a snort and a sniff.

"So, sorry, Inspector," he said, the note of apology by no shadow insincere. "No can do. Absolutely no can do."

Ghote did not attempt to argue. He wished the general good-night, then turned away and marched past the Pathan watchman at the Gardens gate and on down the hill to the still-busy city below.

Next day Ghote made no attempt to telephone Mrs. Amrita Nath, newly appointed Inspector of Smoke Nuisances. Instead he presented himself at her offices and sent in his card with a terse request to see her immediately and urgently.

Somewhat to his surprise he was at once taken up to her office.

The lady he saw at the other side of the wide desk was aged about fifty, sternly stout in figure, wearing a sari of a severe but rich green, with a pair of gold-rimmed spectacles glinting in the middle of a square-set face.

"Now, what is this, Inspector Ghote?" she jabbed out as soon as the peon had shut the door behind him. "I am getting messages from you three to four times a day, and when I am replying that I will return your call in proper time I find you here on my doorstep only."

"Madam, I was already making it clear per telephone that my business is, one, urgent, and, two, confidential."

"Urgent to you it may be, Inspector. But I also have many urgent matters."

"Nevertheless, madam, I am here acting on the orders of the Commissioner himself, on a matter of very great importance."

This must be the third time, he reflected, that he had taken the Commissioner's name to secure himself a hearing. But although he had had no direct indication that his orders came from the top, it was certain enough that they did. Whoever had been made uneasy at last by Freddy Kersasp's activities must be in a position to urge action even on the Commissioner. And as that request had been passed downward it had doubtless grown step by step more forceful.

Certainly, now the mention of the Commissioner's name had its effect. Mrs. Nath gave him a long, assessing look through her sharp spectacles.

"Very well, then, Inspector," she said at last, "state your exact business."

Ghote cursed himself. He had intended to approach the matter of the blackmail Mrs. Nath had acceded to in as roundabout a manner as he could. Because the truth of it was that he was by no means sure what exactly the lady had done to put herself in Freddy Kersasp's clutches.

Shiv Chand had been none too precise.

"Inspector, it is only that when Freddy sahib saw in *Times of India* her name, when she was appointed to that post, he was bursting into a belly laugh itself."

"That only?"

"No, Inspector. One word also he was saying, just only one word."

"And that was . . . ?"

"*Benares*, Inspector. *Benares*."

"That is not at all a help."

"Inspector, perhaps yes, perhaps no. Kindly consider this much. The lady is widow, yes? It was stating in newspaper at time of appointment. Ten, fifteen years past she has lost her husband. Now, Inspector, you are man of world. You must be knowing what is often happening when a good-looking woman is deprived of husband at an early age. Quick-quick like bees to honeypot, the good friends of that departed husband are coming. Anything you are needing, they are asking one and all, yes?"

"Yes, yes. I know what you are meaning. Get on with it, man, get on with it."

"Yes, Inspector. So sometimes, isn't it, six-seven months after husband is expiring lady in question finds addition beginning to come to family? So then it is time for pilgrimage to Benares, no? And not returning home for three-four months after."

That had been the fullest extent of the information he had been able to get out of the shark-smiling Punjabi, dubious as it was. So how was he now to respond to Mrs. Nath's sharp demand to him to state his business?

"Madam," he said, advancing cautiously as a pi-dog approaching a butcher cutting up a goat, "I was informing telephonically, you would remember, that the matter I am wishing to discuss concerns one Mr. Freddy Kersasp, owner-editor of the *Gup Shup* magazine."

"Yes, yes. But what had that man to do with me?"

It was not quite the right reply. If she really had nothing on her conscience, she would surely have sounded more bewildered than she had. He felt heartened.

"Madam," he said, "I think you are all too well knowing. Mr. Kersasp was threatening to print in said *Gup Shup* magazine something to your discredit, isn't it?"

On the other side of the wide desk with its piled files and heaped papers, Mrs. Nath's eyes behind the spectacles with which she faced and intimidated the world wavered.

He felt a swift surge of joy, hunter's joy. Surely now at least he could be certain that he had in sight someone who had suffered at Freddy Kersasp's hands. But would he be able to bring her to the point of standing up in court, as Shrimati X, Y, or Z, and getting her revenge on the editor blackmailer?

"Madam," he said, putting into the words all the authority he was capable of, "I am here to request and require you to give evidence against the said Mr. Freddy Kersasp on a charge of blackmail shortly to be brought. You are cent percent aware that Mr. Kersasp has blackmailed you by demanding an insertion in the book *Indians of Merit and Distinction*. He has blackmailed in similar manner many others also, and now is the time to put one stop to his each and every nefarious activity."

For a long while Mrs. Nath remained silent.

Now with all the ferocity which she had first shown gone,

Ghote decided that there was nothing more for him to do now but to look. To look at her unblinkingly, until she succumbed to the inevitable.

But then slowly—he could see it happening as if a visible movement was taking place—that ferociousness came seeping back into the stout body of the new Inspector of Smoke Nuisances. At last she spoke.

"Many others. You have said, Inspector, that Mr. Kersasp has blackmailed many others?"

"Yes," Ghote replied, if with a small sinking of dismay he was unable to prevent. "Yes, madam, many people have become that man's victims. We are looking to you to lift off from them their burdens and bugbears."

"And why to me only, Inspector?" the sharp voice came back at him. "Why, to a woman only when there must be men, by tens and twenties, who could do what you are asking?"

Despite his premonition, Ghote felt blankly deprived as Mrs. Nath's evident refusal was put so aggressively before him.

"Madam," he stammered. "Madam, there are reasons. Good reasons, I am assuring you."

"And what are they, Inspector, if you please?"

Mrs. Nath was wholly back now to the formidable figure who had greeted him at his first coming in.

"Madam—you see, there are difficulties."

"What difficulties, Inspector? I do not think you were foreseeing too many difficulties in my case. What difficulties do you see in others'?"

Ghote felt he could well understand now how it was that Mrs. Nath had been appointed Bombay's first female Inspector of Smoke Nuisances. It would be a tough mill owner who dared defy her.

He swallowed.

"Madam, there are not so many witnesses we have with good evidences that blackmail has taken place."

"But I am not the only one, Inspector?"

It was a question in form only. And he knew, even as he spoke the words, that the answer he gave to it was feeble.

"It is not always possible for persons, even with the best intentions, to agree to appear in court."

"And so you have myself only, Inspector? And you have come to me, a woman, to help you when no one else was willing to do it?"

"No, madam, no. That is . . ."

"That is yes, Inspector."

Again the blunt statement.

"Well, Inspector," Mrs. Nath went on, turning to one of the piles of papers in front of her with a markedly businesslike air, "I must tell you that I am no more able to help you than any of the gentlemen you have so far asked. Yes, I paid for an entry in *Indians of Merit and Distinction*. But that is something altogether over and done with. Mr. Kersasp would not ask again, I can tell you. You see, when I was a girl only we stayed next to the Parsi colony, Zarina Baag, where Freddy Kersasp was residing, and I am knowing enough about Mr. Kersasp's bad boyhood habits for him not to want me to talk to some other gossip sheet. So, Inspector, I must ask you to let me get on with my work. I have plenty-plenty."

Leadenly Ghote turned to go. He knew when he was beaten. A piece of minor blackmail was keeping Mrs. Nath safe from any more demands from Freddy Kersasp. She must have chosen to use it only when, perhaps, he had talked of a second payment for *Indians of Merit and Distinction*. It had been enough, however. She would pay him no more. But neither would she go to court to give evidence against him.

So what can I say to the Assistant Commissioner? he asked himself as he stood on the pavement outside the offices of the Inspectorate with the heat of the day beating up at him from the dirt-blackened stones. This is the end of the trail. Definitely.

EIGHT

It was only when Ghote was faced with the Assistant Commissioner himself next day, across the expanse of his wide, papers-piled desk with its glinting array of little silvery paperweights each bearing the Assistant Commissioner's own initials, that he realized he had not, after all, come to the end of the trail. Or perhaps not. Not quite.

He had been on the very point of admitting that, after all the time he had spent, he had nothing to report. But then, reliving those last dispiriting moments in the cabin of the Inspector of Smoke Nuisances, he had abruptly realized just what a few words she had thrown at him aside might mean.

When I was a girl only we stayed next to the Parsi colony, Zarina Baag, where Freddy Kersasp was residing, and I am knowing enough about Mr. Kersasp's bad boyhood habits . . .

Perhaps those bad habits had been the bad habits of almost any boy. But if the threat of telling another gossip sheet about them had been enough to keep *Gup Shup* at arm's length, then they were surely more than just boyhood pranks. As a youth Freddy Kersasp must have been a real miscreant. And that was, now he came to think about it, very possible.

After all, if Freddy Kersasp's family came from somewhere no higher in the social scale than the Zarina Baag colony—one of those groups of flats endowed by rich charitable Parsis for members of their community with jobs such as bank clerks and bookkeepers—then the young Freddy would not have had the money to start up anything like *Gup Shup*. That was an altogether glossy affair, and always had been. So its young proprietor must have got hold of finance somehow, and what more likely than by illegal means.

At a colony like Zarina Baag there should be, too, people still there who had known Freddy Kersasp before he became notorious. In crammed and crowded Bombay any Parsi who had decent accommodation at a reasonable rent was not going to leave till they were carried away by the corpse-bearing nasehsalas to the Towers of Silence. So by talking with the very oldest colony residents, with luck he could get a line on Freddy Kersasp's illegalities of twenty-five or more years earlier. Then they could perhaps get him charge-sheeted for something less tricky than blackmail, and that would be the end of him. Which was what somebody up there wanted. As did the Commissioner. And the Assistant Commissioner, Crime Branch.

"Sir," he said, standing at attention in front of that wide, wide desk, "it has been altogether difficult, but I think I see one way to proceed."

Then he outlined his thoughts.

"Very well, Ghote. So what for are you standing here? Get out to Zarina Baag, man, and do some damn digging."

"Yes, sir. At once, sir."

He did not go to Zarina Baag with as much speed as the Assistant Commissioner had required. A little thought had made him realize that to find anyone there old enough to remember the days when Freddy Kersasp, dreaded owner of *Gup Shup*, had been no more than a youth, it would be best to arrive well into the afternoon. Only by three o'clock or after would the oldest inhabitants have woken from sleep in the heat of midday and be ready happily to gossip.

He was right. At a quarter past three exactly, squeezing through the tall rust-bitten iron gate in the heavy stone wall that

surrounded the colony, he saw at once just what he had hoped
for. He had had no conscious plan for getting hold of a likely
source of information, reckoning it would be pointless to
anticipate what he would find. He had hoped simply that by
merely looking about he would come across someone old
enough to remember young Freddy Kersasp. But now, the
moment he had entered the stone-flagged compound of the
baag, his luck seemed to be in.

Sitting in the shade on the steps of one of the four yellowy-
gray buildings around the compound—a faded board above the
entrance proclaimed it as BLOCK D—was an aged man, dressed in
a white bows-tied dugli. Hands folded over the head of an
elaborately carved walking stick, he was evidently telling a story
to a cluster of children on the steps below.

He ought to be ideal.

Strolling round the sun-glaring compound as if unsure which
of the four damp-stained blocks of flats it was that he wanted, or
whether he wanted any of them at all, Ghote gradually got
himself nearer and nearer. At last, after even halting to peer at a
chalk-scrawled cricket wicket on one of D Block's walls—he
would have been hard put to account for the action had he been
questioned—he arrived within hearing distance of the ancient
storyteller. As soon as the tale was over and the children back to
their games of cricket or natgolio—the necessary pile of seven flat
stones stood in a corner of the compound—he was going to seize
on this heaven-sent source of information.

Idly amused, he listened to the tale, remembering boyhood
hours spent drinking in long and long stories he had been told.
It did not take him more than a minute or two, however, to
gather that, ancient though the teller was, his tale was modern
enough. It was an account, nothing less, of a pioneer solo feat of
aviation made in his young days by the millionaire industrialist
J.R.D. Tata. Something designed presumably to rouse in its
juvenile Parsi hearers a stirring of pride and ambition.

Only, as the tale progressed, it became apparent, to Ghote's
increased amusement, that it was by no means a strictly factual
account. J.R.D. Tata's airplane was made to perform some

unlikely, and very daring, feats. And as each one was added, Ghote thought he was able to detect in the old man's right eye—the left was clouded with a cataract—a sharp twinkling of delight in the embellishments that had occurred to him.

At last, with a triumphant and wholly fantastical double loop-the-loop the intrepid aviator was brought safely to land and a garland-wielding reception from every single inhabitant of millions-crammed Bombay. The listening circle, after pleading in vain for "Another, Uncle, another," reluctantly dispersed.

Ghote descended then on his prey like a sharp-taloned kite that had pinpointed from high above a juicy morsel. Only, his swoop was not as free as the bird's of any thought other than of the object below.

Suddenly he had realized that, if his half-blind informant could insert a double loop-the-loop into Mr. Tata's undoubtedly real exploit, then he might well be capable of adding any number of fanciful extras to whatever he might remember about young Freddy Kersasp. But too late now for second thoughts. The old man had begun to push himself up with his ornately carved stick from his place on the top step.

Ghote stepped forward.

Seeing this stranger approaching so directly, the old storyteller let his ancient, rake-thin body happily fold back into a sitting position.

"Good afternoon, sir," Ghote said. "Forgive me for having listened to the tale you were telling those children, but I was finding it altogether very, very interesting. There must be many things about your community in the old days that you are remembering."

He was delighted to find he had hit neatly on a way into the very heart of what he had come to discover. His approach proved to have been exactly what was needed. Quite plainly there was nothing his discovery enjoyed more than mulling over events from his distant past.

Half an hour, almost three-quarters, drifted by. Settling after a while on the steps beside his potential source of information about the young Freddy Kersasp, Ghote was regaled with a scarcely faltering stream of reminiscence. Out beyond in the compound the children shouted and called. Cricket had been resumed at the chalk-scrawled wicket. In the far corner the natgolio ball was flung, retrieved, and flung again. A few of the more enterprising spirits—the Kersasps of some future time, Ghote wondered—tried to evade the watchman at the gate and get to the sugarcane vendor on the pavement opposite cranking his iron mill as he fed it with the inch-thick purply lengths of cane and caught in his heavy, smeary glasses the thick sweet juice that ran out.

But two things spoiled Ghote's feelings of achievement. From time to time he caught in the old man's good eye, plain to be seen, the twinkling he had spotted each time some fantasy had been added to the real exploits of Mr. J.R.D. Tata. And, try though he did more than once, he never seemed able to edge the talk toward events in Zarina Baag itself at the time he was aiming for.

Eventually yet another anxiety entered his mind. For how much longer could such an old man keep up this lively flow? Soon, surely, he would begin to grow tired. He might even in midsentence just nod off to sleep. The very old did that.

"Excuse me, sir," he interrupted almost brutally once more, "but you must have many jolly interesting remembrances of this baag itself, yes?"

The old man gave him a slightly aggrieved look from his one good eye.

"Well, I am not saying that there are not many things I could tell," he answered. "I am, after all, the oldest inhabitant of the colony, eighty-five years, man and boy—if you do not count Mrs. Vacha in B Block and she forgets everything. But never mind all that. What I was recalling when you were breaking in was the time when old Mr. Tata himself, that great Parsi, was building the Taj Mahal Hotel. Kindly let me finish. Young men these days are no more having any manners."

"No. No. Please go on. I am sorry."

There was nothing else to be said. The old man was certainly showing he had an astonishing memory, much of it even of events in the period when Freddy Kersasp must have been a riffraff in the very compound they were looking on at. It would be madness to get on the wrong side of such a fountaining source of information. But would he ever contrive to get him on to the subject of young Freddy Kersasp himself?

The old man grunted in ungracious acknowledgment of his apology.

"Yes, as I was telling, Mr. Tata was building that very-very posh hotel itself because he had been refused admittance else-where on account of not being a white sahib. But . . . but . . . Now, what was I going to say?"

The old man sat blankly regarding an oilwalla who had come pushing his barrel-cart into the compound, singing out his presence, halting from time to time as housewives appeared with containers to be filled.

Oh, no, Ghote thought. It has happened. He is starting to lose his grip. It is the beginning of tiredness. In two-three minutes he will be asleep.

But suddenly the old man broke into speech again.

"Ah, yes, manners. In my day young people in this baag had manners. Things were very different, I am telling. Every single boy in the colony was altogether polite to elders. Never any— No. No, I am wrong. One there was who was not at all polite."

He paused and shot Ghote a new glare out of his one unclouded eye, as much as to say that here was another clearly failing in manners.

But who was the one boy he was recalling who had been not at all polite? Could it possibly be Freddy Kersasp? But why should it be? After all, the old man might not even be thinking of that particular time. His wandering mind might have flipped back to half a century past. Or to only ten or fifteen years earlier. Yet . . .

"You have heard of one Mr. Freddy Kersasp? Now owner of that notorious magazine by the name of *Gup Shup*?"

Ghote could scarcely bring out a sound indicating he knew what the old man was talking about. Happily the choked gasp he produced seemed to be enough.

"Now there was one who was all the time causing utmost trouble," the aged storyteller went on, with every sign of being thoroughly embarked again. "Do you know what he was once doing? I will tell. He was—he was—he was kidnapping the dastur we had then, a very holy man. Yes, he took prisoner a priest and held him to ransom. Every family in the baag had to pay rupees ten before Dasturji was let go."

Was this it? Was this what Mrs. Nath had known to Freddy Kersasp's discredit? And would it possibly be enough to charge-sheet him with after all these years?

Ghote's mind raced.

Until it was borne in on him that in the single bright eye in the old man's face beside him there was, distinctly, a twinkling. Then, guided by some instinct, he looked away across the sun-battered compound, milling now with the various vendors permitted to enter, the vegetablewalla with his cry of "Onions one rupee the kilo," the fishwalli with her basket of gleaming pomfrets, the man who exchanged old clothes for cheap metal bowls. And there, just turning out of the gate, was a Parsi priest, a dastur, wearing the flowing white garb of his profession, bearded to the waist as laid down by religious ordinance.

Should he indicate to the old man at his side that he knew perfectly well now what had put that fantastic kidnapping story into his head? If he did, would it so offend him that he would refuse to say another word? Just at the point he had cajoled him toward for a solid hour? But, if he refrained, how could he ever be sure that what he might learn about Freddy Kersasp's past was in any way the truth?

He gulped.

"Oh, sir," he said, "that is one very, very good tale. One hundred percent joke. But this Mr. Freddy Kersasp, he was also truly doing wicked things in his youthful days?"

He waited, not daring so much as to breathe, for the response.

The one unclouded eye in the time-creased face beside him twinkled yet more brightly.

"Well, well. Perhaps, telling tales to the young ones so often as

I do, I have allowed something of the fairy story to come in. Yes. Yes, something of the fairy story."

"But there are things about Mr. Freddy Kersasp in his youth that are not at all fairy story?"

For a little—for what seemed to Ghote almost to be long hours—the old man did not reply. A beggar who had sidled his way into the compound was loudly calling, "Firstfloorwalla bai, feed the poor. Secondfloorwalla bai, give and get blessing." The heat seemed to be springing up even more throbbingly from the uneven paving stones in front of them.

At last the old man answered him.

"Do you know, my dear sir, that many years ago here in this baag itself there was a murder?"

A murder. Could it be— No, surely, this was too much to hope for.

"Well," the old man added quite hastily, "I am saying murder, but perhaps it was something less than that."

"Less?"

Was the old fellow retreating now from some contemplated fantasy? Was his "murder" going to turn out to be something no worse than Freddy Kersasp giving some other boy one black eye?

"Yes. You see, what was happening was that a gentleman then living in the baag, one Mr. Topiwala, the former owner of a sandalwood shop close to our big Parsi fire-temple behind Girgaum Road—very successful business with all the worshipers wanting to buy before going to that agiary . . . Well, Mr. Topiwala had become a notorious miser in his retirement. In his flat, so it was said by one and all, he was keeping untold wealth. And then one day he was robbed. Every rupee, every anna. And afterward he was found dead. In the end the police were giving out that it was just only case of heart attack caused by fearful distress of event. But, after all, that is not so much different from murder."

"No," Ghote agreed, his mind racing once again. "No, it is almost as bad as murder itself."

But was the old man saying that Freddy Kersasp had been that murderer, or near murderer? And, if so, would it be possible after all the years that had gone by to bring the crime home to him?

"Sir, that is altogether most interesting," he said. "And is it that you are telling that Mr. Freddy Kersasp, now known to one and all as *Gup Shup* proprietor, was that selfsame robber?"

"Robber?" the old man said, with a sudden sly look. "What are you asking about robber? I was telling story of Taj Mahal Hotel, yes? That they are saying and slandering that it was by mistake built wrong way round. Well, I tell you, sir, if that is what you are thinking you are well . . . and truly . . . mistaken. Yes, mistake . . ."

Then what Ghote had earlier feared might happen, that the ancient storyteller would be overcome by sleep, seemed to have occurred. His good twinkling eye and his clouded one closed. His head sank toward the hands clasped over the ornate head of his stick.

Or was he feigning sleep? Was he getting out of having once again fallen into the self-made trap of introducing fantasy into a factual account by pretending to have forgotten what he had been saying? And had he capped his ruse with this pretense of sleep?

He looked at the bony, white-clad figure hunched on the steps, head lolling.

There was no telling. And if the man had truly lapsed into sleep, it would be heartless to wake him. Nor would he in all likelihood remember what it was that he had been talking about. Even if he was pretending sleep, he would, forced back to the light of day, evade either confirming or denying what he had said. That could be taken as certain.

What to do?

He could, possibly, call at the local police station and see if they had records going back as far as he needed. But he hardly had enough to go on to guide him. No definite date. Only one name, that Mr. Topiwala, former proprietor of a shop selling sandalwood to pious Parsis wishing to feed the sacred fire in their agiary. It might take weeks to dig out the facts of the robbery in the course of which Mr. Topiwala had been murdered, or had died. And even if he found the records, it was by no means certain that Freddy Kersasp in his youth had had anything to do with the case. There was only the old man's abrupt reference to the robbery after Freddy Kersasp's name had been mentioned to indicate there was any link at all.

There might, too, of course, be other very old inhabitants of the colony who would remember the Topiwala case. Perhaps it would only be a matter of going about until he found someone ancient enough to have remembered. But would any one of them know as much as this old man sleeping beside him about Freddy Kersasp's connection with the affair? After all, it cannot have been common knowledge, or the young Freddy Kersasp would have been arrested and charged with the crime.

But then had the owner of *Gup Shup* really been connected with the business at all? Or had that been yet another of the old storyteller's flights of fancy? And anyhow it was not going to be so easy to discover another informant going back as far and with as good a memory apparently as his first lucky find. He had certainly seen no one else of the same sort in the time he had been here. So would it be a matter of going around knocking at every door in the baag and asking if there was any very old person there? That, again, could take days if not weeks. And in the end he might find no one with a really good memory of those distant days.

He sat on the steps next to the old man snoring with a soft sizzling sound beside him and gave way to sudden rolling waves of frustrated misery. What a damn complicated business had been thrust on to him. And all, when you came down to it, because of that other blackmailer, dead Dolly Daruwala. If she had not tried to gather into her icy net Dr. Commissariat, that fine man and benefactor, then he himself would not be sitting here, trying to make sense of the senseless fantastical ramblings of an ancient Parsi and under orders to find evidence with which to charge-sheet for some offense, for *any* offense, the man half of Bombay—or half of influential Bombay—dreaded and feared.

What a first-class bloody mess it all was.

NINE

The strip of shade in front of Zarina Baag's D Block moved quarter-inch by quarter-inch down the steps where Ghote and his aged sleeping source of information sat side by side. The children playing natgolio finished their game amid a sharp outbreak of quarreling. The beggar seeking leftover food from the wives of the firstfloorwalla and the secondfloorwalla moved on to A Block. An eggs vendor arrived and added his cry of "Hen eggs, English eggs" to the various other sounds of the compound. The oilwalla, sales finished, began pushing his cart toward the gate.

And, quite suddenly, Ghote realized that he did after all have a way forward that promised to get him the quick result the Assistant Commissioner himself was under pressure to produce.

The old snoring fellow beside him was not, he had actually himself admitted, the oldest inhabitant of the baag. That was a woman. What had her name been? She came from B Block, yes. That much he remembered.

And, yes . . . yes, she was a Mrs. Vacha. And when the old man had declared that she had "forgotten everything," there had been a definite underlayer of jealousy in his voice. So was Mrs. Vacha, in fact, a rival to him as the keeper of the traditions and anecdotes of life in the colony? It might be. It very well might be. Yes, she would definitely be worth going to see.

He jumped up.

His arm had brushed against the aged figure sitting beside him, eyes lightly closed, head lolling, bony hands resting on the head of his stick. For a few moments the old man rocked to and fro sideways till it looked as if he might topple over. But then the motion ceased and he remained lost in slumber.

So that sudden attack of sleepiness had been genuine after all. No matter. The old man and his memories were no longer vital. In all probability a source of information as good or better awaited.

He ran, despite the still-battering sun, across the compound, dodging one of the cricket-playing boys running for the ball. Inside the hallway of B Block he saw, to his abruptly sweat-running relief, a painted board bearing the names of its tenants. And, at the top of it: MR. AND MRS. D. VACHA.

There was a lift at the back of the coolly dark hallway. He hurried over.

LIFT IS TEMPORARILY OUT OF ORDER. The words were written in very faded ink on a sheet of paper stuck between the bars of the gates, crisp and buckled with age.

With a sigh he turned to the yet-darker well of the stairs. It seemed a weary tramp up, even though it was no more than three floors. But what made it more sapping of the spurt of hope he had experienced when he had realized this Mrs. Vacha might well hold in her head, more to be trusted than the old storyteller's, the very facts he needed was an uprush of recollection. Into his mind there had flooded again the memory of tramping up the many, many more flights of the stone stairs of Marzban Apartments on his way, weeks ago, to Dolly Daruwala's flat. What had happened there had been something that had struck at the whole edifice of his beliefs. Was something almost as bad somehow lying in wait for him now?

He stopped on the second landing, more to beat down that premonition, groundless though it surely must be, than to regain breath. But standing letting such black thoughts sweep over him was not going to get him anywhere.

He braced his shoulders and marched up the remaining flights to the third floor. And there on one of the flat's doors was a small wooden plaque saying, again, MR. AND MRS. D. VACHA, though Mr. Vacha, he suspected, must be long dead.

There was a bellpush at the side of the door. He put his finger to it and pressed.

At first he thought from the still silence that followed that his luck must have run out already and that Mrs. Vacha, despite her age, must be out visiting. But, just as he was about to turn away, having counted to a hundred—the flats after all could not be very large—but then to another hundred just in case, he heard from the other side of the door the laborious slap-slap of someone wearing chappals very slowly approaching. He did his best to adopt a quietly sympathetic expression and waited.

Inside, he heard the door bolt slowly being wriggled open. Then there was another lengthy delay. He imagined Mrs. Vacha, infinitely aged, a mere wraith scarcely still present in the world, pausing to rest after her fluttering labors. He increased the sympathy in his expression till he felt his face creak with it.

At last the door opened.

An enormous woman stood on the far side. She was old, certainly, even very old. But it seemed as if she had devoted all the years she had been alive to increasing layer by layer her girth. Her body was one immense balloon, swathed in the white that Parsis of the older generation so often wore, right up to the scarflike mathoobanoo with which she had covered her head and the fat round tire of chin below it. From her finely wrinkle-covered huge moon of a face there sprouted, here and there, curling white hairs.

A great waft of eau de cologne rolled out from her toward him.

But, he noted with a dart of pleasure, the eyes in the enormous head were, despite the lady's age, bright and black with intelligence.

"Madam," he said, realizing suddenly that for all his long wait for the door to open he had prepared no excuse for wanting to talk. "Madam, I . . . I am . . ."

Then he thought that there was perhaps nothing for it but the truth.

"Madam, I am a police officer, Inspector Ghote by name, and I am making inquiries about the activities here in this baag as a youth in days long gone by of one Mr. Freddy Kersasp."

"Firdaus."

For a moment he failed to understand what she had said. Then it struck him.

"Yes, yes. One Firdaus Kersasp, sometimes known as Freddy."

"Come."

He wondered whether Mrs. Vacha, from extreme old age or from her mere immensity, had difficulty in producing more than a word or two at a time. Perhaps he was not going to find it as simple a matter as he had hoped to confirm from her that a murder, or a death following a robbery, had taken place in the colony when Freddy Kersasp had been a youth on the verge of manhood. Or that it was possible that Freddy, or Firdaus, had been involved, however little the police at the time had been aware of it.

Meanwhile Mrs. Vacha had begun to work her huge, white-clad bulk around with the evident purpose of letting him in, and he suspended judgment. At last she got herself pointing in the right direction and began to move forward, lumberingly and hesitantly as a buffalo at the full span of its days. At each step a chappal softly slapped the floor in a slow, irregular rhythm. Anxiously he followed.

"Bad."

The word emerged like a tiny explosion from the cautiously progressing balloon in front of him.

He felt a bounce of hope. Surely that word, isolated and minimal though it was, must refer to Freddy Kersasp in his early days here in the baag.

It was a supposition reinforced as the trembling inflatable preceding him maneuvered herself along past the open door of her kitchen—it looked too narrow ever to admit her, though the

gas stove on its table and the wide washing mori down at floor
level both looked well-used—and uttered one more puffed-out
syllable.

"Lewd."

But this was followed almost at once by two words of
explanation.

"Dirty remarks."

"Fred— Firdaus Kersasp as a boy was cutting dirty remarks?"

"Always."

So perhaps that was all Mrs. Nath, new Inspector of Smoke
Nuisances, had had to flourish against the owner of *Gup Shup*.
But with Freddy Kersasp's present-day status, it might well have
been just enough. The question was, though, whether young
Firdaus had once done worse than make lewd jokes. Whether,
possibly, he had robbed the retired sandalwood merchant, Mr.
Topiwala, and left him for dead.

Mrs. Vacha had now contrived to squeeze her tremulous bulk
into the flat's living room. Following, Ghote saw against every
wall cupboards and boxes and chests, more almost than he could
count. Each was thickly dust-layered and safely fastened with a
dangling padlock. On such parts of the walls that were left free
there hung heavily framed photographs of past Parsi worthies,
grave-faced men with large moustaches wearing the same puggrees on their heads as he had seen in the two dark oil portraits
in Mr. Z. R. Mistry's drawing room.

At the thought of his meeting there and its consequences, he
felt again an upswelling of chaotic despair. The world was full, it
seemed, of blackmail and blackmailers, each exploiting some
fellow creature. And he himself was among them, threatening
that Muslim locksmith to make him forge the keys to Dolly
Daruwala's flat, and even as a boy—something he had contrived
for years until recently to blot from his memory—promising to
tell on that pencil thief Adik Desmukh.

He experienced a renewed jab of determination to find some
offense other than blackmail to use to put the owner of *Gup Shup*
out of circulation. Something uncontaminated by that virus.

"Mrs. Vacha," he said urgently, "do you remember anything

about Firdaus Kersasp to his detriment more shameful than the uttering of lewd remarks? Do you know even anything about the death in suspicious circumstances here in this colony many years ago of one Mr. Topiwala?"

"Firdaus was doing that."

The huge old woman stood puffing and trembling after the effort of producing the brief accusation. But Ghote dared not show her the consideration he would have liked to have done.

"You are definitely stating and accusing that Firdaus Kersasp in his much younger days was responsible for the death of that man?" he asked demandingly.

"Everyone knowing."

"But Firdaus Kersasp was not arrested. Was he so much as questioned?"

"Questioned and questioned he was. But police are fools."

Ghote decided to ignore that.

"But," he said, "if Firdaus Kersasp was questioned and then let go, there cannot have been one hard-and-fast case against him."

"He was doing it."

The firm accusation had seemingly exhausted the immense old woman. She looked about her, took a faltering pace backward and fell in a huge white heap into a broad armchair, which from its sagging seat showed every sign of having been frequently subjected to such treatment over the years.

For a second Ghote wondered whether his eager ferocity had been altogether too much for his ancient witness. But he saw that the bright black eyes in that huge, wrinkle-skinned face were alert and alive.

"Why are you saying and saying the boy was guilty," he punched out at her then, "when he was never at all charge-sheeted? Why?"

For a little while Mrs. Vacha did not reply. But Ghote suspected this was because she simply lacked the breath. The eyes in her vast face under the white mathoobanoo were shining still.

At last she answered.

"Everyone said . . . was always round at that flat. Demand-ing money. Knew . . ."

"What knew? What?"

"Mr. Topiwala. Secret vice."

Ghote decided this was a line he did not need to pursue. No doubt long-dead Mr. Topiwala had had some vice he wanted no one to learn about. But all he himself needed to know was that Freddy Kersasp had apparently been blackmailing him over whatever this was. Because it would follow, if what Mrs. Vacha was remembering had any shade of truth about it, that the young Freddy had known that the retired sandalwood merchant had money available. The young blackmailer eventually must have pressed too hard, and when Mr. Topiwala had rejected him at last—in the true Duke Wellington way—Freddy had resorted to outright robbery.

Yes, it was all decidedly likely. Only, why had the police at the time contented themselves with questioning only?

He must find out why, if he could.

"Madam," he said, "you have been very very helpful. But may I kindly ask one thing more? Are you remembering what year it was that the late Mr. Topiwala was robbed and died also?"

"Married," Mrs. Vacha puffed out from her wide armchair.

"Married? You are saying that Mr. Topiwala was married? But what has that to do with his death in the end?"

He felt suddenly furious. Furious and baffled. Why had it all become so muddled just when he was on the point of getting it clear?

But Mrs. Vacha, speechless, was pointing to one of the photographs on her wall, a small and smudgy one that hung all on its own in a narrow space between two of the tall, dark padlocked cupboards.

Ghote looked at her, still angrily puzzled. She continued to hold up a gross tubular, trembling arm and indicate the one photograph and nothing else.

He went over to the gap between the cupboards.

And then he understood. The photograph was of a wedding pair. Plainly Mr. and Mrs. Vacha, although she was barely half her present size and he was a dried-up, late-marrying bridegroom if ever there was. But the point of her directing him to the picture

was at once evident. In small golden letters on the foot of its
frame a date was inscribed. A date in May thirty-seven years
earlier.

This must be when the Topiwala robbery had happened. It
would be something Mrs. Vacha could not have forgotten if her
marriage had taken place at much the same time.

"Madam, thank you. Thank you, madam. You have been one
hundred percent helpful. Please do not attempt to show me out.
I can most easily find my way."

Head fluffily swirling with pleasure, Ghote blundered from the
flat and down the dark stairs.

No, he reflected, his fears on the way up had proved ridiculous. Far from meeting with some new unguessable disaster, he
had come away with something real and hard and damn useful.

He hurried, despite the thickly amassed afternoon heat, to the
police station from which, all those years ago, the robbery at
Zarina Baag would have been investigated. Sticky with sweat
both dried and fresh, he introduced himself to the station house
officer. Would their records extend back thirty-seven years?

"Oh, God, yes, Inspector, as long as station itself has been here
records are there. Kindly help yourself."

The sight that confronted him in the station's records room, a
long black place lit only by a strip of small windows close to its
ceiling, soggily stuffy and smelling of long-accumulated musti-
ness, was grimly daunting. He experienced a strong desire to give
up his hunt before he had even begun.

But somewhere among the files and papers stacked in bundles,
two and even three deep, on the slatted wooden shelves that ran
all around the walls and continued in long islands in the center,
there might be a case diary relating to the death of one Mr.
Topiwala at Zarina Baag. The thought drove him to brace
himself and plunge in. If he could discover somewhere in the
daily notes that investigating officers had to enter in a case diary,
by standing order, something to use even now against Freddy
Kersasp, any labor would be worthwhile. Had that blackmailer
not brought death in Delhi to Mr. Ramesh Deswani? And more
than likely death or black misery to many others as well?

He found after a little poking about that the stacked files were at least in chronological order, more or less. So inside half an hour he had actually located the year he wanted. But even as he heaved down the heavy, date-labeled bundle of papers, it began to crumble in his arms.

White ants, he thought. The whole damn lot has been invaded by white ants.

Swiftly he lowered the floppy, fragments-shedding bundle to the floor. Then, sitting cross-legged beside it, he prised open the time-hardened knots of the tape, colorless with age, that bound it.

His surmise proved accurate. File after file in the bundle simply disintegrated as he attempted to pick it out. In minutes he was surrounded by tiny ragged paper pieces like wind-heaped piles of fallen petals. Across such sheets that remained more or less intact the ants' perforated trails wound haphazardly. Here and there their droppings made darker stains on the faded brown to which the ancient sheets had long ago been reduced.

He sneezed violently, once, twice, three times.

Even the cardboard covers of the case diaries he found among the files in the ruined pile—they were a different shape from the ones he was used to, but he recognized them for what they were at once—had, he saw, been mined to pieces by the relentless mandibles.

Misery welled up in him once more. So near yet so far.

But the mound was not yet wholly sorted through. Wrinkling his nose and shutting his mouth tight, he plunged in again. One more case diary came to light, but even as he read the words on its cover the whole fell to bits in his hands. He plucked out one last likely cover. Yes, it too was a case diary. Even the date of the year he had so looked forward to immersing himself in was easy to read. But at least half the book was simply paper crumbs. Cautiously he turned one by one its remaining half pages, alert for the words *Zarina Baag*, or *Topiwala*, or even half of them. But at last he came to the final one. Nothing.

Wearily he eased himself to his feet, gritting his teeth at the pain in his thighs. And then he saw it. At what would have been the very bottom of the tape-bound pile before it had been ant-eaten to so much rubbish, there was the by-now-familiar cover of yet one more case diary as they had been in those distant days. It looked, too, as if, perhaps because of its position at the bottom of the bundle, the ants had largely failed to get their destructive little jaws into it.

He swooped, painful legs forgotten.

And, yes, it was almost totally intact, and the date on it was right. He opened it.

It was at once evident that the first case it happened to have dealt with all those years ago was the Zarina Baag affair. There, written not once but time and again, was that name Topiwala.

In triumph he bore away the slim book, from which all but the bottom pages once under carbon sheets had been long ago torn out. With a brief apology, he settled himself at a corner of the station house officer's table and avidly began to read.

Very soon he found himself feeling more than a little admiration for the officer who had investigated the affair, one Inspector V. P. Lavande. He was splendidly conscientious. There could be no doubting that he had made his entries, as per regulations, each and every day, which was more than some harassed officers did nowadays. Even his handwriting was beautifully clear, and he had pressed with such firmness on the top sheets that the carbon copies were as easy to read as if they had been made just the day before.

Then he came across something infinitely better than the name Topiwala: the name Firdaus Kersasp. Inspector Lavande, it seemed, before his investigation had been more than a few days old, had heard talk about young Firdaus's relations with Mr. Topiwala of the "secret vice." In decency he had at that early stage gone no further into what that vice had been than Ghote had himself. But no sooner had his suspicions been aroused than he had taken Firdaus Kersasp down into the station's detection room for interrogation.

His record of that was as meticulous as all the rest of his notes. After going through the first page Ghote realized he had in front of himself an almost word-for-word account.

Surely now he would find something. Something with which, never mind how many years had gone by, he could pin the crime at Zarina Baag on to Mr. Freddy Kersasp, now proprietor *Gup Shup*.

Only why had Inspector Lavande, that exemplary police officer, not been able to charge-sheet his suspect at the time?

Before very long he found the answer. Freddy Kersasp, or Firdaus as he was called then, almost as soon as Inspector Lavande had begun questioning him, had been indignantly anxious that his imminent departure to England for "higher studies" should not be delayed. It appeared that he had paid for his passage—in those days by ship not plane—well before Mr. Topiwala had been robbed. So he could not have got hold of the necessary money in that way. Nor, it seemed, had he obtained the sum by blackmailing the retired sandalwood merchant, as rumor in Zarina Baag had held. Mr. Topiwala, according to the inspector's scrupulous notes, had been accustomed to keep a daily account with a running total of his hoarded finances, and there had never been any deductions from that total beyond the very small amounts Mr. Topiwala allowed himself for food and other unavoidable expenses. Inspector Lavande had gone back years, till well into the time that Freddy Kersasp would have been a mere Standard V schoolboy, in his meticulous checking.

So, after all, Ghote recognized with twisting irony, at least as a youngster Freddy Kersasp had not been a blackmailer, whatever he had come to be in later life.

He remembered now, too, from the inquiries he had made about the owner of *Gup Shup* that he had as a young man gone to the U.K. Freddy Kersasp had always stated, apparently, that it was there he had acquired the money to start up his magazine. Back in those distant days his parents, he had explained to Inspector Lavande, had borrowed the passage money he had needed. Even that Inspector Lavande, admirably conscientious as ever, had confirmed with old Mr. Kersasp, bookkeeper on minimal salary at a place called the New Laxmi Paper Mart. Firdaus's parents had held a modest party for their relatives to see off the boy some days before the Topiwala robbery had occurred, though he had not departed then.

From all this Inspector Lavande had decided that the Kersasp line led nowhere. It was a conclusion that Ghote found he could only agree with.

Once more he was left with nothing to go on.

Next day—it was well on into the evening now—he would have to have yet another session with Shiv Chand and see if that shark-smiling Punjabi could after all rake up just one other name in the tally of those who had paid for insertions in *Indians of Merit and Distinction*. But this was a faint chance at best, and there was always the danger that Shiv Chand would put him on to some influential citizen who had genuinely sought admission to the as-yet-unprinted prestigious volume. If he went to one of them hinting they had done something to lay themselves open to blackmail he would be—

He spoke the words aloud.

"In one hell of a soup."

Doing all that he could to fight off the deep depression his afternoon's fruitless work threatened, he made his way home. Perhaps next day Shiv Chand would produce a perfect witness he had hitherto not so much as even remembered, one ready and willing with only the merest hint to go into the witness box under the guise of Shri X. Or perhaps Freddy Kersasp himself would have heard some rumor about what was happening and would have decided that enough was enough and have returned, forever, to America. Perhaps. Perhaps.

But more likely than not, he said to himself darkly, he would arrive home to find the squinting, sidling figure of Ranchod waiting for him, hand held out for another hundred rupees. He had come last time several days before a month had been up, and had been yet more slyly urgent in his demand.

But to his relief there was no one outside his door. He tapped in his customary manner and in a moment heard Protima unloosing the door bolt.

The comforts of home. The prospect of showering away the sweat and the filth of the white ants' destructiveness, of sitting and relaxing—he would ask Protima to press his feet—of the evening meal bubbling with delicious spiciness on the stove began to lift his gloom.

"Well," Protima said as soon as she had opened the door, "I have some news."

Somehow he knew it would be good news. It had to be. He could bear nothing else now. And besides, Protima seemed quietly pleased.

"Yes?" he said. "What news it is?"

"It is Ved. He has bought his home computer."

He felt himself assailed by conflicting emotions. First, since Protima seemed so delighted, he tried to feel equally pleased. But then also he was considerably puzzled. How could the boy have acquired enough money to pay for a computer? And had he got it legitimately from Vision Radio and Computer Service? Or had he bought it, smuggled, from a pavementwalla at Flora Fountain? But if he had done that, why was Protima still pleased? And then did he himself actually welcome Ved getting the thing at all? Such an outlandish, modern object?

He even detected in himself a tinge of jealousy. How had it somehow come about that Ved, his little Ved, knew about computers when he himself was hardly aware of anything more than that they existed? They were there, mysterious, useful no doubt, but altogether in the realm of the unknown. And now his son—his son—seemed to be very much at home with them. And had bought one.

Ved had bought a home computer when he himself had said the very word was not to be mentioned under his roof.

He found he was standing deprived of speech just outside his own door. And, as much as anything not to show Protima that the arrival of the computer had put him into this state of bewildered perplexity, he stepped briskly inside.

"Well, well," he said with assumed loud confidence, "let me see this great new thing we are having, yes?"

Ved appeared at the doorway of his room.

"You have it inside?" Ghote asked. "You are keeping this big-big thing to yourself only?"

"No, Dadaji."

"It is going to sit with us, then? Poor old television is to be sent into kitchen, one hundred percent in disgrace, yes?"

"No, no, Dadaji. You are having to use screen of TV with home computer."

Ghote felt a flicker of anger coming to dominate the conflicting emotions the news had sent swarming up in him.

All right, he had got it wrong. But how was he to know a home computer used the TV screen? Why should he be some expert in electronics all of a sudden? If *electronics* was the word he meant.

"Well, well," he said, rasping with sarcasm, "so none of us is to be allowed to watch TV anymore, is it? So your mother will have to give up every Sunday morning the Mahabharata when that so holy program is meaning so much to her she is even taking bath before it? And your father, will he have to go without knowing what is happening in world because news in Hindi or English cannot be seen?"

"No, Dadaji, no."

"I am glad to hear."

Ved in the doorway of his room seemed to be having the grace to look a little ashamed. He scraped the side of his bare foot along the floor.

"Computer is not here," he said. "Yet."

"So? When it is coming? When is flat to be made into twenty-first-century temple only?"

Ved looked even more abashed.

"I am having to pay still," he muttered.

And at that Ghote's half-suppressed rage flared into full flame.

"So that is your idea," he shouted. "Trying to make me agree to damn thing by saying it is bought already when you have laid down not so much as one rupee for it. That is blackmail, my son. Damn bloody blackmail. And you will suffer for it. I will be teaching you one lesson you will not ever be forgetting."

"Husbandji," he heard Protima faintly protesting.

But his rage, which he knew had been fed as much by the frustrations of the day behind him and, beyond those, all the

troubles that had assailed him ever since the evening he had been
sent to see Mr. Z. R. Mistry, was not to be appeased.

Furiously he looked around to see if he could find something
with which to beat his son as he had never been beaten before.
And in a moment he spotted one of the boy's chappals where he
had kicked it from his foot as he had gone into his room. With
anger-fueled strides he marched over to it.

But then, at the very instant he bent to pick it up, something
in his head let in a cooling gust of unexpected enlightenment.

I would teach the boy to be jumping the gun like that, he had
been thinking in thick rage. And suddenly he had realized that,
only a few hours earlier, he had equally encountered somebody
who had jumped a gun. Young Firdaus Kersasp. Firdaus Kersasp
had told the world that he had booked a passage to the U.K. for
his "further studies" well before the robbery of Mr. Topiwala's
hoarded fortune. But there was no real reason why in advance of
committing a robbery he had long planned he should not have
pretended to book that passage. Or even have got hold of a
temporary loan actually to book it. Later, when Inspector
Lavande's inquiries had come too close, he could have persuaded
his father to say the passage money had been provided by
himself, swearing to him he was innocent and saying he feared
for his place at that college in the U.K. if police inquiries delayed
his departure.

He let Ved's chappal fall almost as soon as his hand had
grasped it.

TEN

Next morning, first thing, Ghote requested an interview with the Assistant Commissioner. When he was summoned, something over an hour and a half later, he laid out, briefly as he could, his theory about how the young Firdaus Kersasp had provided himself with a sort of prealibi before robbing Mr. Topiwala, the crime that had led to the old sandalwood merchant's death.

"Yes," the Assistant Commissioner said when he had come, a little breathlessly, to a halt. "You may well be right, Ghote. I am inclined to think you are. Yes, right enough. But we would need somewhat more before we try tackling Mr. Freddy Kersasp."

He sat behind his sweep of a desk and pondered.

Ghote, standing to attention in front, was careful not to interrupt the process. At last the Assistant Commissioner spoke.

"Yes. Well, if what you suspect is correct, then the money Kersasp used to start up that appalling publication must have come not from some magazine he is supposed to have run in England but from what he stole from that Parsi recluse of yours. What's his name?"

"Topiwala, sir."

"Exactly. The money must have been what Mr. Topiwala had made from the sale of his sandalwood business. A good deal, no doubt. Say what you like about your Parsi, he's a damn good businessman."

"Yes, sir."

"Yes. It stands out a mile. All that stuff about his early days Freddy Kersasp is always writing in that column of his must be the sheerest fabrication."

"Please, sir, what stuff is that?" Ghote asked.

"Don't you read the rag, Inspector?"

"No, sir. Never have, sir."

"Yes. Well, my wife— That is, the damn servants sometimes bring copies into the flat. Suppose it's my duty, in a way, to keep an eye on it."

"Yes, sir. Of course, sir."

"Well, thing is, Kersasp keeps claiming that during his sojourn in the U.K. he started up some damn magazine to do with Indian arts and made a hell of a success of it. And the fruits of that, he has the bloody impudence to say, he brings to the task of correcting the ills of society here. Says he does it only for the sake of India itself."

"Yes, sir."

"So he's got to be stopped, Ghote. And I venture to think I've seen the way to do it. Now, if the fellow didn't make that fortune of his in the U.K. as he claims, we ought to be able to get evidence for it. Damn it, if that magazine there never existed or was no more than some wretched sheet nobody wanted to buy, then we can quickly enough find out. I'll have a message sent to Scotland Yard ek dum. They'll provide an answer in no time at all. And when we find that claim of Kersasp's is all bunkum, as I personally am willing to bet, then we'll have every bit enough to tackle the fellow with."

"Yes, sir."

Clicking heels in salute, Ghote left the Assistant Commissioner's cabin. In his heart he cherished the thought that, thanks to something he himself had hit on, the tremendous machinery of distant Scotland Yard was going to be set rapidly to work.

The Assistant Commissioner's faith in the swiftness of Scotland Yard inquiries proved to be misplaced. As days, and then weeks, went by Ghote took it on himself to ask from time to time whether an answer had arrived. And after a while he thought it wiser not to ask.

Work on cases mercifully with no tint of blackmail to them kept him busy. He had one satisfying triumph when, thanks to recalling that it was a custom among Sindhis to offer guests from their own community crisp and spicy papads as a snack with any drinks, he deduced that the visitors who had murdered a Sindhi businessman must be of Sindhi origin themselves, and had then been able to trace and arrest them. And he had a good many days of frustration in trying to get a line on some distributors of "brown sugar," the crudely processed heroin that was becoming a menace on the Bombay streets.

Before long he even began to feel that the whole miserable period of his life that had followed his visit to Mr. Z. R. Mistry was going to slide into the past, become simply a time to be looked back on, and that as infrequently as possible. Even Inspector Singh, he gathered, had moved on to other matters than the Dolly Daruwala murder, for all that the affair had not been officially relegated to the files.

Eventually it was only the visits Mr. Mistry's Ranchod continued to make that kept an uneasily prickling consciousness of blackmail in his mind. Ranchod's demands, though he had come to feel them as no more than one of the irksome routines of life, were, however, becoming little by little more frequent. Where at first they had been strictly once-a-month affairs, now the fellow was appearing certainly at two-week intervals. He seemed each time, too, to have a more unpleasant air about him. He had developed a habit of drooling at the mouth, or was no longer taking pains to control it, and even his squint appeared to be getting yet worse.

But on the other hand he felt it safe now in response to

Ranchod's outthrust hand to say firmly that he would get no more than fifty rupees. Once even, toward the end of a month when funds were short, he made it as little as twenty-five, confident from the look of pleading in the fellow's eyes that he would be satisfied with even that much.

Yet he could not bring himself finally to give him the Duke Wellington answer. The payments he made him were not a tremendous drain on his resources. By cutting down on one or two little luxuries—he stopped altogether buying paans to chew from the brass-bright stands of the vendors—he could pretty well make up the money. And it was worth making absolutely sure such a figure as Dr. Commissariat—the TV news still sometimes showed him standing in front of some impressive piece of apparatus in his new laboratory—remained untouched.

Then one day, nearly three months after the Assistant Commissioner had sent his message to Scotland Yard, the phone in Ghote's cabin rang and he heard the familiar brisk voice ordering him to come up.

"You sent for me, sir."

"Ah, yes, Ghote. Ghote. Now what . . . ah, yes. Scotland Yard. Well, they have turned up trumps, as I always said they would. You can trust the British to get things done, Ghote."

"Yes, sir."

"Yes."

The Assistant Commissioner riffled through the papers on his desk.

"Ah, yes, yes. Here it is. Short and sweet. Short and sweet. Listen to this, Ghote."

"Yes, sir."

"No trace any periodical owned or managed by Frederick, otherwise Firdaus, Kersasp."

"Then, sir, it must be certain Mr. Kersasp was acquiring the money to start up *Gup Shup* from that robbery in Zarina Baag."

"That's it, Ghote. Told you so in the first place. Shady customer, Kersasp. Always was."

The Assistant Commissioner sat back in his broad chair.

"Now, this is what we'll do, Ghote. In point of fact, so many years after the event there's precious little hope of getting a case that would hold water in court. We know that. But Mr. Freddy Kersasp can't be altogether sure how much we might be able to do. So, it's perfectly simple. We go to him, and lay our cards on the table. Some of them. We make out that we've got his best interests at heart. And we say: Get out of India while you can, or we would not be able to hold back full investigations. That ought to do it."

Yes, Ghote thought, that may very likely do it. It may very likely achieve what whoever up there spoke to the Commissioner in the first place is wanting done: putting an end to *Gup Shup* and its nasty allegations and those costly entries in *Indians of Merit and Distinction*. But all the same it is one thing only: blackmail.

"Yes, Ghote," the Assistant Commissioner said, his voice purring as a fish-fed cat's. "So, no time like the present, yes? Make an appointment with Mr. Kersasp straightaway."

"Sir, me?"

"Yes, Ghote, you. You. You don't expect an Assistant Commissioner of Police to go doing that kind of dirty— To go asking to see someone like Mr. Freddy Kersasp, do you?"

"No, sir, no."

"Very well, then, get on with it, man. Get on with it."

"Yes, sir."

Ghote took it upon himself, however, not to carry out the Assistant Commissioner's instruction to the letter. He calculated that for a task as delicate, and alarmingly difficult, as he had been given, it would be necessary to choose the very best time and place. It would be madness, for instance, to go to the offices of *Gup Shup* at this hour of the morning and attempt in those surroundings to—to blackmail Freddy Kersasp. There was no other word for it.

So he spent some time reviewing everything he had learned about the owner of *Gup Shup* from its dismissed office manager, still awaiting trial on a charge of extortion under Section 383 of the Indian Penal Code. And eventually he came to the conclusion

that the best moment to make his bid would be, in fact, at the
end of that very morning. Because this was Wednesday.

Every Wednesday at the Ripon Club it was the custom to serve
at lunch the great Parsi dish, dhansak. And every Wednesday,
Shiv Chand had said, Freddy Kersasp was accustomed to set out
from the *Gup Shup* offices at precisely half past twelve to walk to
the club, there both to savor the dhansak and show himself to the
cream of the Parsi community in all his dangerous glory.

To fall in beside Freddy Kersasp on that walk—"He is
progressing there as if he was King-Emperor only," Shiv Chand
had snarled—might well be the best moment to conduct his
awkward negotiation without any witness. Now that he himself
had to play the blackmailer, he was not going to make Shiv
Chand's own mistake at the Taj Mahal Hotel.

So in good time he stationed himself a couple of hundred
yards away from the *Gup Shup* offices and waited.

And, just as Shiv Chand had said, to the minute there appeared
King-Emperor Freddy Kersasp. At once Ghote saw why the
bitter Punjabi had applied that expression to his former boss.
Freddy Kersasp was an undeniably impressive figure. From his
shock of prematurely white hair to his thickly jutting white
eyebrows, to his wide and curly white moustache, on down to his
solidly puffed-out, white-shirted belly over which there flowed a
wide, colorful, striped tie, he exuded rosy self-confidence.
Among the weaving hundreds making their way here and there
or nowhere on the pavement, he was probably not particularly
noticed. But, silver-headed shiny malacca cane grasped in one
hand like a scepter, he acted as if every eye was upon him. It was,
indeed, a royal progress.

Ghote pulled back his shoulders and thought of the Assistant
Commissioner. He had been ordered to do what he was about to
do. He was acting, in fact, with all the implied authority of the
Commissioner himself, however much what had been asked of
him was—no hiding it—blackmail. And however little, if things
went wrong, he would get any backing from above. That much
he knew without having to think about it.

Now the sailing, self-confident figure was almost upon him.

He felt a lurch of apprehension but nevertheless stepped boldly forward.

"Excuse, please. It is Mr. Freddy Kersasp?"

Freddy Kersasp did not show, by the least flicker of his eyes or turn of his imposing white-haired head, that he was in any way aware of the approach.

Ghote's heart sank. Was this how the dreaded figure dealt with unexpected introductions? No doubt in the course of his battening career he had had some nasty encounters with those he had threatened. So did he ignore any stranger now entirely? And would he be able to get away with it? Sweep triumphantly past? Progress all the way to the sacred portals of the Ripon Club and there, surrounded by witnesses, be safe from all demands and threats?

And then he saw it.

From Freddy Kersasp's left ear there dangled a silky black wire. The cord of a hearing device. Like many Parsis, then, he must suffer from deafness. Deafness in one ear at least. And it had been on the deaf side that, by chance, he had made his approach.

Careless of dignity, he scuttled around behind the slowly progressing, cane-twirling figure, took a skip and a jump to get just in front of him, and tried again.

"Please, it is Mr. Freddy Kersasp?"

And the King-Emperor graciously answered.

"That is, as it happens, my name. What can I do for you, my dear sir? It is some charitable request? Alas, I am well-known through all Bombay as what is called a soft touch."

"No, no. It is not at all that."

"Then what is it, my dear chap? I am a busy man, you know. I have appointments. Appointments."

Freddy Kersasp, who had deigned for a moment to halt his progress toward the Ripon Club and its steaming, spicy dhansak, started to move away. But then, abruptly, he stopped and turned to face Ghote directly. The white projecting eyebrows beneath his shock of white hair contracted into a sharp frown.

"I don't know you," he said. "You are not, I hope, someone

attempting to complain about something I have written in my magazine? Because if so are I must warn you . . ."

He shifted his grip on his heavily knobbed malacca stick.

"No, no," Ghote said quickly. "It is in no way such. It is that I am wishing to speak with you as a friend only."

Freddy Kersasp began now to turn away again.

"As friend," Ghote added, rapidly throwing in an extra lie, "and as a very, very great admirer of your *Gup Shup* column itself."

It was enough to make Freddy Kersasp transfer his cane in an instant to his other hand and swiftly to capture Ghote's arm with his own.

"Recognition, my dear sir," he said, for all Bombay to hear if they cared to listen, "is welcome. Always welcome. You may be surprised to hear it. You may think that a person like myself, a writer like myself, will have had his surfeit of recognition. But, no. No, a modicum of praise is ever welcome."

In face of that, Ghote was unsure how to go on. But again he thought of the Assistant Commissioner and what it was that had been required of him.

He swallowed as, marched onward by the buoyantly sailing Freddy Kersasp, he became aware of how much nearer, even in a minute or so, they had got to the gates of the Ripon Club and all those there who must not hear a police officer practicing nothing less than blackmail.

"Sir," he said, "what I have to tell is altogether one hundred percent urgent."

"Ah, information," Freddy Kersasp exclaimed, at once freeing Ghote's arm. "I thought somehow you were not a person . . . However, no matter. I regard it as my duty to receive information—however disgusting, however revealing it may be of the ills of our present-day society. Speak, my dear fellow, speak."

But then he came to a halt once more, the briefest of halts.

"One thing however," he said, raising a warning hand. "Not a single paisa. I do not pay, my good sir, to be told the tittle-tattle of the sewers of society. Though if what you are good enough to

inform me of proves satisfactory, there may be a small honorarium. A small honorarium."

He resumed the royal progress.

"Speak, my good fellow, speak. Do not hesitate. Not a word
goes any further."

But now Ghote was experiencing a healthy crackle of revulsion
at the blatancy of the *Gup Shup* blackmailer's tactics.

"Sir," he said sharply, "it is not at all a question of information
for the pages of your—"

He managed to check the savage description he had been
about to apply.

"What I am telling," he went on, letting an edge of authority
have full play in his voice, "is that you yourself are in very much
of danger."

"Danger? My dear chap, Freddy Kersasp has faced danger
enough in his time. Do you think I carry this stick simply for
show? I tell you—"

"No," Ghote broke in, pretty well convinced by now that in
fact Freddy Kersasp did carry his silver-headed stick for show.
"No. Do not be thinking your danger is in any way something
that a few blows from a stick will be saving you from. Mr.
Kersasp, you are in danger of finding yourself arrested for one
cognizable and nonbailable offense."

Once more Freddy Kersasp came to a halt. Fleetingly Ghote
wondered whether the fellow's Wednesday progress toward his
dhansak lunch had ever been so often interrupted.

"My good man, I do not know what you are attempting to tell
me. But let me make it clear to you. Freddy Kersasp has been in
danger of arrest on more occasions than he can count. But once
only has he ever set foot inside a court, and then he emerged in
triumph. In triumph, sir."

"But that was on a charge of extortion only," Ghote snapped
back.

And now Freddy Kersasp's broad, white-eyebrowed, white-
moustached face took on, for a single instant, a look of fear.

"Who the devil are you?" he shot out.

"I am a police officer, Mr. Kersasp. But one who is your friend only."

"My friend, are you?"

"Yes indeed, Mr. Kersasp. And that is why I have taken the chance to speak with you altogether in private."

Slowly Freddy Kersasp threaded his arm through Ghote's once more.

"Yes, my dear fellow?" he said, setting out in the direction of the Ripon Club once again but at a noticeably slower pace. "Now, tell me everything. You say you have enjoyed my column in *Gup Shup*? Is that the only reason you are being so good as to—to warn me?"

Ghote was tempted to make this the moment when he came out with the real reason why he was telling Freddy Kersasp about the threat hanging over him. But he decided that the pretense might be worth carrying on a little longer.

"Oh, yes, sir," he said. "I would not at all like to see a person of your—of your very great cleverness being put on trial under Indian Penal Code Section Three-seven-eight."

"Section Three-seven-eight? What on earth is that?"

"Sir, it is theft."

"Theft? Theft?" Freddy Kersasp broke into a giant laugh. "Well, I have been accused of many things in my time, but I never expected to hear myself called a common thief. Thank you for your kindly warning, my dear sir, but I think you have got hold of the wrong man."

"No, sir."

"No? Come, my good fellow, enough of this."

"No, sir. The theft you are very, very likely to be accused of was occurring at a Parsi colony by the name of Zarina Baag some thirty-seven years past."

For the fourth time Freddy Kersasp stopped in his tracks. A renewed look of fear came on to his bluff face. And stayed there longer than an instant.

"What are you saying?"

"Mr. Kersasp, I am saying the whole truth. Police inquiries in recent weeks have led to the utmost suspicion that it was you and you alone who was responsible for a certain robbery of one Mr. Topiwala at Zarina Baag those many years past, and that perhaps the death of the said Mr. Topiwala can be laid to your door also."

"And how the devil do you know so much about that? What's your name? You've been pretty careful to keep that under the table."

"My name is Ghote, sir. I am an inspector of Crime Branch. But there is a colleague of mine, one by the name of Inspector Arjun Singh, and it is that man who has got upon your track itself."

Feeling a dart of pleasure at the swiftness with which he had put, so to speak, a mythical Arjun Singh between himself and his still-formidable opponent, Ghote gave Freddy Kersasp a long, steady look.

"Well, Inspector Ghote," the owner of *Gup Shup* said slowly, "let me thank you for the warning you have seen fit to give me. But let me also point out to you that this crime, this alleged crime, took place nearly forty years ago. And what is more it happened when I was on the point of leaving for higher studies in the U.K., where incidentally I later very rapidly prospered as a magazine owner. Editor and owner, as perhaps you may know."

"No, sir, you were not at all prospering in that line in U.K. We have received Scotland Yard information to that effect."

Again a look of alarm appeared on Freddy Kersasp's face.

"But—but—" he said. "But I could not have taken that old man's money so as to get to England. I had paid for my passage long before that robbery took place."

"No, sir. That would not wash also. There was no reason why you should not have borrowed money to secure your passage and at once paid back same from part proceeds of robbery."

"But my father, Khoedai rest him—"

"No, sir."

Freddy Kersasp's tongue appeared beneath his luxuriant white moustache and licked at his lips.

"Well, Inspector," he said after a little while, "as I was saying, it is good of you to tell me all this. But I do not believe on reflection that I am in any real danger. No one is going to bring a prosecution after so many years. And I have friends . . . friends."

"Sir, you have also enemies."

"No, no, my good fellow. Freddy Kersasp may have said some harsh things on occasion about certain people, but that was necessary. Necessary to cleanse the Augean stables of this country. A phrase of which I have often, alas, had to make use."

Ghote looked at him.

It was plain the shock of hearing that his long-ago crime was once again being actively investigated had rapidly worn off. He had even turned in the direction of the Ripon Club once more, and was lifting his head as if the odor of dhansak was already in his nostrils.

"Mr. Kersasp," Ghote said, "let me assure. Enemies you have and are having. Let me speak one hundred percent frankly. I am not such a friend to you as I was giving myself out to be. You may say that I am one of those enemies. I would add only this. A great many people would be altogether happy if *Gup Shup* was no longer appearing and you were no longer staying in India."

Freddy Kersasp turned his face away from the distant odor of dhansak.

"By God, that is blackmail," he said. "You damn swine, you are attempting to blackmail me."

"Call it whatsoever you are liking," Ghote answered, finding in himself suddenly a tiny writhing of pleasure in the game he was playing. "Whatsoever you are calling same, it is not making anything of difference. The one fact is that if *Gup Shup* is continuing to appear, then investigation of crime at Zarina Baag will continue to be made. And I am promising evidence will be found to put you behind the bars once and for all."

Freddy Kersasp stood where he was on the pavement. Past him to either side the citizens of Bombay—beggars and hawkers, businessmen in their cool suits, astrologers, coolies, sharp-smelling fishwallas in their gaudy, tucked-up saris, Hindus, Muslims, Christians, and Parsis—went by in all their variety. At last he spoke.

"Very well, Inspector. I have been at the game you are playing too long myself not to know when I am beaten. You, and those I do not doubt who give you your orders, want to see the back of Freddy Kersasp. Isn't that it? Well, I suppose I must let you have your way."

He lifted a hand to the black cord of his hearing-aid as if it no longer mattered whether he was able to keep in touch with the life around him or not. But even this gesture seemed in the end to be too much for him. His hand fell to his side.

Ghote, however, felt not the least spark of pity for the suddenly old man. Far from it. A sharp exultation seemed to be running in his blood.

"Well," Freddy Kersasp said in face of the unmoved silence that confronted him. "I will see about shifting to New York or somewhere as soon as I can manage to wind things up here."

"No, Mr. Kersasp."

Ghote was almost surprised to hear himself saying the words. But something from deep within him had leaped commandingly into the saddle, and he could no longer control the onrush he felt.

"No, Mr. Kersasp," he repeated. "You will go now, this instant, to Air India office and book one ticket for first available flight. I myself will communicate with the said office telephonically at 5 P.M. precisely, and if I am not hearing you have booked the flight I will set in train every possible investigation."

Now Freddy Kersasp simply turned away. His shoulders were bowed. His shiny malacca cane trailed in his hand.

Ghote, watching him go, wondered to himself. He had blackmailed the fellow. There could be no other word for it. He had been in possession of a fact to Freddy Kersasp's disadvantage, and he had used it to the utmost to force him to do exactly as he had wanted. Or exactly as he had been given orders to get him to do. But, he realized, the fact that he had been acting under orders had been no excuse. He had enjoyed doing what he had done. Yes, in the end he had enjoyed it. To see Freddy Kersasp humiliated and beaten had given him intense pleasure. Nor was the fact that Kersasp was a thoroughly criminal fellow any excuse again. Whatever the man he had had at his mercy had been, villain or one as much practicing "good thoughts, good words, good deeds" as Dr. Commissariat himself, he would have revelled in having him under his thumb. Squirming.

He thought suddenly of his schoolfellow of old, Adik Desmukh. Yes, he had for a time felt just such an icy pleasure in having big Adik wriggling under his knowledge of that stolen pencil. And he was feeling that pleasure still as he watched Freddy Kersasp walk away beaten.

But nevertheless he had done it. He had pulled it off. He had sent Freddy Kersasp—there could be no doubt of it—packing.

ELEVEN

By the time Ghote had returned to headquarters to report his success to the Assistant Commissioner, he had managed to push back into the deep recesses of his mind all the unpleasant pleasure that he had taken in blackmailing Freddy Kersasp. The Assistant Commissioner's evident satisfaction at his news left no room in any case for anything but a feeling of rich contentment. Only briefly was a shadow cast on that by the notion that luck might have played some part in his triumph.

What if Freddy Kersasp had held out against me, he thought at one moment. How on earth then would I ever have succeeded to get rid of him and his bogus and spicy magazine? I could not have killed the fellow. I could not have turned myself into a Dr. Commissariat and eliminated a vermin, pest, and snake.

But the thought hardly impinged. Within seconds it was submerged by another great wave of pleasure in what he had accomplished. The Commissioner himself had indicated that it was time Freddy Kersasp's nefarious activities were brought to an end. Someone up there, indeed, must have surely indicated as much to the Commissioner. Finally he, Inspector Ganesh Ghote, had been given the order. And, within hours, he had carried it out. Freddy Kersasp had announced his intention of giving up his game, and there was no doubt he would do it.

He buzzed with inner happiness.

It was a state that was to be deflated abruptly as soon as he reached home that evening.

Ranchod was the cause. He found the squint-eyed servant, as he had discovered him on occasion after occasion since the murder of Dolly Daruwala, waiting in the shadows outside his door. His first thought, as he realized the fellow was there, was that this visit was at an even shorter interval than any before.

This time I will damn well send him about his business, he thought. Dr. Commissariat must be safe by now. Months have passed, after all. Arjun Singh is on the tracks of altogether different no-goods and criminals. Now at last I must be able to give this damn fellow the true Duke Wellington answer.

He swung around to deliver it.

But Ranchod, sidling quickly up toward him, saliva drooling from the corner of his mouth, spoke first.

"Rupees one thousand. I must have it."

Ghote could not believe what he had heard.

"What—what it is you are saying?"

Ranchod held out a filthy hand—how can Mr. Z. R. Mistry tolerate such a dirty fellow, Ghote thought—and advanced one more sidling step nearer.

"Rupees one thousand," he repeated. "Give now, or I would tell and tell what I was seeing."

Ghote hardly needed to think.

"No," he said. "No, damn you, get out of my sight before I kick you down the stair."

Ranchod gave him one look, a piteously imploring look he was to realize soon afterward, and then, without a word, he turned and at a shambling half run headed for the stairs.

For a little Ghote stood there without giving his customary tapping signal on the outer latch of his door.

Have I spoiled everything after all, he asked himself suddenly. Is my Duke Wellington answer sending the fellow even now to his nearby police station, going over in his mind just what he will say there? Was I wrong to think time has made Dr. Commissariat safe?

Has one angry word brought the end of that great man? And for me also? Will I, tomorrow or the next day, find a fellow from Vigilance Branch coming to my cabin, asking and asking questions I cannot answer? And Dr. Commissariat, will he find the handcuffs round his wrists? Be dragged into the cells? Come up for trial? Be hanged even? Is that what the Duke Wellington answer brings about?

A shiver of cold ran through him from throat to stomach.

But at once he told himself not to be foolish. Time had passed, and in any case Ranchod was not truly likely to go to a police station. It was difficult to imagine that drooling, jittery figure persuading a station house officer that he had such important information.

Then, in an instant of illumination, he realized why that was.

Yes, yes, he said to himself, a fellow so altogether lacking the guts to enter a police station, with so much of drooling and slobbering. He must be an addict only. Yes, it must be brown sugar itself that has all along been his weakness. That has been the reason he has been making his demands more and more often, begging and beseeching. He has been more and more badly needing money.

For a moment he wondered whether he should chase after the fellow and make him say where he was buying his supplies. Might that lead back to the ring now making so much headway selling brown sugar on the streets?

But, no, he thought, there is not much hope of getting to the mastermind behind the gang through a fellow like Ranchod. They would take good care he is not even knowing the name of the man he is buying from.

With a sigh he turned and tapped at the door.

And in any case, he thought as he waited for Protima to come and draw back the bolt, with that habit of Ranchod's tomorrow at this very time I would quite likely be finding him here again.

In that, he proved to be mistaken. Neither the next evening nor on any one after did the squinting servant put in an appearance, hand outstretched for brown-sugar money. Gradually as the days

went by the black boulder that had loomed up in his mind as he
had seen Dolly Daruwala fall with a thump dead to the floor
receded further and further into the mistiness of time.

Nevertheless for weeks after rejecting that sudden and unexpected demand for a thousand rupees, as he arrived home each
evening he continued to look with a touch of apprehension into
the dark corner where Ranchod had been accustomed to lurk.
But then one night he realized that he had not given that spot his
quick, habitual scrutiny for the past two or three times. Once or
twice in the succeeding days he remembered again to make his
check. But even as he did so he felt sure he would not see in the
darkness any hunched, stooping shape.

Eventually he decided, however, that finally to set his mind at
rest, he would have to go and take one last look at Ranchod. He
would have to venture to observe him on his home ground. At
Marzban Apartments, at Mr. Z. R. Mistry's flat.

He was not very happy at having even to go near the place. For
one thing he feared a visit to the actual spot at which an event so
overwhelming had happened to him would once again call up
feelings he would find every bit as hard to deal with as he had in
those moments he had stayed lying under Dolly Daruwala's bed
knowing he was letting a murderer go unchallenged. The black
boulder, which he really believed had all but disappeared into the
mists, might suddenly lurch horribly to the front once more. And
there was the possibility, remote and even ridiculous though it
might seem, that somehow his presence there would even now
light a powder trail fizzing back at last to Dr. Commissariat
himself.

But his niggle of doubt about Ranchod would not, despite
these thoughts, vanish. So at last, carefully choosing an hour
when he thought it most likely that Ranchod would be coming
out of Mr. Mistry's flat, duties for the day over, he set off for
Marzban Apartments.

He turned out to be luckier even than he had hoped. No
sooner had he hidden himself in the soft darkness outside the
block—to his intense inner discomfort in the very place he had
waited before breaking into the flat that night long ago—than he

saw Mr. Mistry himself leave the building. He knew at once what he would do: ring at the doorbell of his flat and then rapidly slip out of sight. When Ranchod came to answer, if he was there, he would be able to get a good look at him, see whether he had been right about the brown sugar, see whether the fellow was still inclined to drool at the mouth, see if he looked contented with his lot once more. He would get one last good look at him. Then he would be able to lay these fragments of his fears to rest once and for all.

He came boldly out of hiding, nodded with assurance to the chowkidar on duty in the foyer of the tall block, and then went, while the man could not see him, and rang at Mr. Mistry's familiar, unpleasantly familiar, bell.

No sooner had it rung than he darted back into the farthest corner of the lobby, where it was every bit as dark as he could have wanted.

After less than half a minute the door of the flat was opened and a beam of light shone out. But the servant who had answered was not Ranchod. Squinting Ranchod he would have recognized in an instant anywhere. This was an altogether different individual. Tall, stooping, suspicious-looking. But, clearly, Mr. Mistry's servant. Dust cloth over shoulder, white or whitish uniform cladding his gaunt body.

So Ranchod was no longer in Mr. Mistry's service. And the fellow was no longer making those rupee-requesting visits. Perhaps, the thought came to him, he had even died. Brown sugar claimed its victims all too often, all too soon.

For a moment he felt a twinge of pity. But Ranchod had, after all, been nothing but a blackmailer. He hardly deserved pity.

He took a deep breath where he stood in the dark and watched the suspicious servant close Mr. Mistry's door with a grunt of weariness.

So it is over, he allowed himself at last to think. Ranchod has left the scene. Definitely. That nightmare at least is finished and done with.

As if to confirm his new-found relief, the very next afternoon he bumped into Inspector Arjun Singh, avoided for so long.

"Ghote bhai," the energy-bouncing Sikh greeted him. "Days and days since I have seen. Where you been hiding? I was wishing to say good-bye."

"Good-bye?" Ghote echoed stupidly, still wondering at the edge of his mind whether he ought to have kept out of Singh's way in case the talk somehow got into the dangerous area.

"Yes, yes, man. I am shifting."

"Shifting? It is that you are leaving Bombay?"

"No, no, bhai. I would not do that. Action is here. But job change I will take, both hands grabbing."

Ghote by now felt on safer ground.

"What job change?" he said. "You have been in Crime Branch ten minutes only."

"Two years, bhai. Two whole years. Time to move on, no?"

"Well, myself I have stayed here longer. But where to are you shifting?"

"Vigilance Branch, bhai. Not so far away. So one naughty move from you when I am there and I would be eating your head only."

The big Sikh exploded into a roar of laughter.

For a moment Ghote returned to his fears that one day squinting Ranchod, not after all dead, would tell what he had seen on the stairs that now distant night in Marzban Apartments and a Vigilance Branch investigation would descend on him. But, as quickly, a different thought replaced that retrospective twinge of anxiety. If Singh was transferring to Vigilance Branch, it meant that he would no longer in any way be pursuing, lionlike, Dolly Daruwala's murderer. The case, though no doubt still nominally under investigation, had in effect finally been allowed to be forgotten.

Breathlessly he shook the Sikh's bear-paw hand and wished him "Best of luck only." Then he sought the refuge of his office and, sinking into his chair, he wallowed for a while in luxurious contemplation.

Now at last Dr. Commissariat, for all that he had never known what danger he was in, could go about his good work safe from any menace whatsoever. Now I, too, he said to himself, can go about my work safe and sound, and not have to fight down any thoughts that each day may be the last I am allowed to do it.

In the days that followed the process of burying those last doubts was much helped because he had more than his usual piled-on amount of work to do. The Commissioner, relieved perhaps of his anxieties over *Gup Shup* with the departure of Freddy Kersasp for America—Ghote had had to go to Sahar Airport and actually witness him stepping into the plane—had some time before launched a tremendous drive against infractions of the Maharashtra Prevention of Dangerous Activities of Slumlords, Bootleggers, and Drug Offenders Act. He wanted, so rumor at headquarters had it, to show up Bombay Police's rival, the Directorate of Revenue Intelligence. Their success not long before in making a haul of 103 kilograms of brown sugar, valued at no less than thirty crores of rupees, from "a shop-cum-residence" in the suburb of Dadar had gained considerable newspaper notice.

Above all, the Commissioner and the Assistant Commissioner, Crime Branch, under him wanted a stop put to the activities of a certain underworld kingpin who had recently moved from gambling and protection rackets into brown-sugar distribution, one known as Uncle, or Mama, Chiplunkar. And it was for the operation against him that Ghote had found extra duties by the dozen put on his plate.

Mama Chiplunkar had, embarrassingly, long been well-known for his activities to Bombay Police Intelligence Branch. But in spite of all the information they had succeeded in collecting about the gang he ran, nothing had ever been found to put him behind bars. It was said that this was more than likely due to Chiplunkar having a source somewhere inside headquarters, repeatedly tipping him off.

It was a fact certainly that the crime kingpin was able to go about Bombay—he described himself as a "social worker"—with, in the words of a *Sunday Observer* story highly critical of the police, "fanfare and impunity." A short time before, however, he had in fact had a narrow escape in a raid on a beer bar managed by one of his right-hand men, and it was this that had perhaps made the Commissioner believe his moment had come.

So, though hours at work were long and arduous, life for Ghote became once again serene. It was even, he thought occasionally, an extra blessing that the drain on his finances made by his regular payments to Ranchod had come to an end. Every now and again he caught himself wondering how he might spend the savings he was making. His scooter had been giving him trouble—it was well past its first youth—and he let the vision of himself riding to and from headquarters on a brand-new one tickle the back of his mind.

But then one day another demand on his more comfortable resources presented itself. An unexpected demand. He had had a particularly hard twelve hours fruitlessly trying to track down a minor hanger-on of Mama Chiplunkar's believed to be someone who if leaned on hard enough might prove a lead. "Each drop that is added toward positive results makes a milestone ulti-mately," the Assistant Commissioner had said.

Coming home exhausted, he thought he detected in Protima a certain, well-hidden uneasiness. He decided, tired as he was and not sure how capable he would be of any tactfulness that might be necessary, to wait before he tried to find out what it was all about. But Protima spared him the trouble.

No sooner had he finished eating than she returned from taking his thali to the kitchen holding in front of her a piece evidently torn from a newspaper.

Without a word she placed it on the table. He looked down at it.

"What it is?" he said. "It is seeming to be some 'For Sale' advertisements only."

"Yes, yes. Read. Read where it is marked."

Feeling a prickle of suspicion, he nevertheless did as he had been asked. A small pencil line had been put against one of the advertisements in the column.

It was for a secondhand home computer.

Rage, fueled by the residue of his tiredness, sprang up in him.

"Home computer, home computer!" he barked. "Have I not said and said such a thing is not to be mentioned in this house?"

"But I am not mentioning," Protima answered with a infuriating little smile. "I am showing you newspaper ad only."

"And who was marking this?" he demanded. "Who? Who? If it is Ved, I would—I would . . ."

"Of course, it was Ved," Protima answered. "Are you thinking I would notice such an ad itself? But the poor boy is wanting and wanting still to have home computer, and I was just only finding this newspaper he had marked."

"What if he is wanting and wanting? Home computer is one hundred percent too expensive, and I do not wish to see such a thing under my roof ever."

"But, husbandji, it is no longer very much expensive. Look at what that advertiser is asking."

Ghote glared at the figure, hardly seeing it.

"Oh," he snapped, "and are you thinking I am able to lay down such a sum at any minute? Am I Mr. Tata himself that I should have crores and lakhs to throw?"

"Husbandji, it is not crores and lakhs. It is rupees three thousand only. A good sum, I am granting. But perhaps not too much for us to find. And the boy has been so good. He has not once tried to trick you into getting him what he is so much wanting, not after you were ordering him to silence. And—and—"

"Yes? What and? What more now?"

"And it would be very, very good for him to have such a thing, I am thinking. It would help him to learn to use these computer-tooters. And even now he is always mugging and mugging at physics. This would give him one very good career in future."

For long, long seconds Ghote glared down at the ragged strip of newsprint in front of him. Then he found that he was thinking, with a sharp pang of regret, about the new scooter—he had seen a Bajaj advertised at sixteen thousand rupees—which he had dimly contemplated possessing. It was this that did it. When it came to it, he knew he would almost certainly not feel able to

buy for himself something hardly absolutely necessary in place of
an object a good deal less costly that Ved had set his heart on.

And, besides, the boy had been good. He had never again tried
his blackmailing tactic after the time he had so narrowly escaped
a beating. And if perhaps now he had practiced a little cunning,
a little chalak, in the way he had let his mother come upon the
advertisement he had marked, well, that showed only how much
this twenty-first-century object meant to him. Then to have a son
who was a computer engineer . . .

"We would see," he grunted out.

And, lying in bed that night, he began working out a sort of
account of how much he was saving by not having to pay
Ranchod. Then he started calculating how far away that total was
from the three thousand rupees needed for the secondhand home
computer, though before he had managed to bring the two
columns together sleep overtook him.

Early next morning, however, he was to discover, disastrously,
that all his mental arithmetic had been so much waste of effort.

He was setting off for headquarters, standing in the road
attempting to fire the motor of his scooter, seemingly yet more
troublesome than usual, kicking and kicking ever more venge-
fully at its starting lever. Then, just as the motor did at last give
out two gun-shot splutters before fading into sullen silence once
more, a voice spoke from behind him.

"You should have one altogether new."

He felt a dart of fury, all the more bitter for his hardly yet taken
resolution not to save for a new machine in favor of getting Ved
the home computer.

Who was this damn stranger to tell him what or what not he
was needing?

He swung angrily around.

And found out who the stranger was. A man he had never met,
but one who had been carefully pointed out to him from a
distance. Mama Chiplunkar.

There could be no mistaking him. A chubbily fat fellow,
dressed in a creamy-white silk kurta and pyjama, with a round
face and scanty hair, well-oiled, spread across his skull. He was

smiling grinningly, a splay of big teeth, red-stained from much paan-chewing, bright in the fresh morning light.

Ghote was astonished. What was this man doing here now? This kingpin and mastermind who had been in his official thoughts almost ever since that terrible Freddy Kersasp business had come to an end?

"What?" he shot out. "It is Mama Chiplunkar. Mama Chiplunkar."

Mama Chiplunkar's big smile widened even farther.

"So glad you are knowing," he said. "Because there is some business I am wanting to talk."

"Business? Business? What business can you be having with me?"

"Well, Inspector," Chiplunkar replied easily, a new smile splitting his round face, "I suppose you might call it blackmail business."

TWELVE

Astonishment hit Ghote like a giant monsoon wave. He took an involuntary step backward. Behind him his scooter crashed to the ground. He ignored it.

"What it is you are saying?" he challenged the chubby, smiling gang boss. "You are saying you are intending to blackmail me?"

Mama Chiplunkar smiled yet more broadly.

"Yes, yes, Inspector," he said. "Listen, if I am telling what I am wanting you to do for me, in one moment you would be shouting, 'But that is blackmail only.' So why not say that out loud now, first of all? You would be calling it blackmail. I would call it business only. But whatever it is called is same thing."

Ghote stiffened himself up.

"And I am able to tell you," he said, "business or blackmail, call it what you are liking, I want nothing to do with same."

"Oh, but Inspectorji," Mama Chiplunkar replied, unperturbed, "you are not having any choice."

"But I am. I choose to say to you no."

Mama Chiplunkar wagged his head cheerfully.

"No, no, Inspector. Let me tell you, I would not have gone to trouble of finding out where you stay and of coming here early-early in the day itself if I was not certain you must be doing what I ask."

"No. You have wasted your time only."

But the brown-sugar kingpin's unvarying assurance had set up in Ghote an inner dismay that made that answer something only a little less than bluster.

What could a man like this possibly know about him that would allow him to think he could exercise blackmail over him? There was nothing in his life, thank God, that made him open to—

Then he thought of Dr. Commissariat.

But how could Mama Chiplunkar possibly know anything about those few terrible minutes in Dolly Daruwala's flat? Even Ranchod, now disappeared for good if not dead, had been able to do no more than work out that there had been somebody in that flat at the time of the murder, somebody unknown he himself was protecting. No, there could be nothing, nothing, to give this swine a hold over him.

Mama Chiplunkar's face broke into another wide horseshoe smile.

"Inspector," he said. "Let me say one name only, Inspector: Ranchod."

At once Ghote knew that, altogether unlikely though it seemed, Mama Chiplunkar must have been an acquaintance of Mr. Z. R. Mistry's servant. And, worse, far worse, he must have learned from him what he had seen on the stairs of Marzban Apartments the night Dr. Commissariat had put an end to the existence of vermin, pest, and snake Dolly Daruwala.

But, aware that the situation was for whatever reason hopeless, he yet tried to show himself as uncomprehending.

"Ranchod? Ranchod?" he jabbered. "That is one common name. What should it be to me that you are mentioning some Ranchod?"

"Oh, come, Inspector. This is one business matter we have to talk. Kindly treat it as such only."

"But I am knowing nothing of any Ranchods."

Mama Chiplunkar sighed.

"And yet this same Ranchod, until some weeks ago the servant of one Mr. Z. R. Mistry in a posh flat in Marzban Apartments on

Malabar Hill, was visiting you month by month and you were
handing over to him the sum of rupees one hundred each time."

The final tatters of Ghote's hope went streaming away in that
cold wind.

"What—what are you wanting?" he heard himself ask.

"That is much-much better," Mama Chiplunkar replied. "Now
we can be discussing business-business."

"Yes?"

For a moment Ghote thought how, hardly two minutes earlier,
he had said so defiantly that he wanted nothing to do with any
business or blackmail proposition Mama Chiplunkar might
make. But what could he do now, in face of even the little the
fellow had shown he knew? Nothing but kowtow to the man's
superiority and hear what he had to say.

"Let me tell you first what it is you are wanting," Mama
Chiplunkar went on smoothly. "In business it is always best for
each side to know what is wanted by the other. Then matters can
be finished with no lyings and trickeries."

He actually waited, apparently for Ghote to agree.

"Go on. Yes, yes."

"Good. Now you are seeing things the right way, Inspector,
just as I was hoping."

A tiny spark of revolt flew up in Ghote at this assumption that
he would be such easy prey. Flew up, and died in the air.

"Yes, let me tell you," the gang boss continued, giving a quick
glance up and down the road, beginning not to be busy with the
earliest office-goers. "That Ranchod was a great liker of card-
playing. But a great fool at it also. So he was losing and losing
money, to many friends of mine. But, foolish, foolish fellow,
when he was owing so much he was resorting to, first, charas to
forget all his troubles, and after some time when charas was
seeming too mild to him he was going to brown sugar itself.
Then when he was, by one great piece of luck, getting steady
extra income—"

He leaned forward and stuck a pudgy forefinger into Ghote's
ribs.

"Then when he was getting this nice-nice extra income, what

was he doing but deciding he could take more of brown sugar. Very, very catching habit brown sugar, yes, Inspector?"

Ghote knew that he had to agree with the blatant hypocrisy, even if it was only by so much as a nod. But it hurt to give that nod. Hurt savagely.

"Yes. So quite soon that foolish Ranchod was needing-needing more and more of brown sugar. And more and more of money to pay for same. And then—oh, toba, toba—whoever was giving his extra income said finish. So what was he to do? He was so badly and badly needing. You have seen addicts when they cannot get their supply, Inspector?"

Ghote thought of the people he had occasionally come across in the worst distress of deprivation of the drug. The shaking, shivering, and sickness, the slobbering and drooling, the dagger pains that so plainly afflicted them.

"Yes," he grated out. "I have seen."

"So what was the poor fellow to do but to come to me, a known and famous social worker?"

Mama Chiplunkar's smile broke widely over his face more.

"And to me," he went on, "Ranchod was telling his each and every trouble. What he had seen one night in Marzban Apartments, the police inspector who was keeping a big-big secret, all, all. So what must I do? Out of kindness of heart itself, I am keeping the poor fellow safe and sound in a place I have got. How could I let him go into the streets only when he is so addicted?"

The smile left his face like a light switched off.

"Now this is what it is you are wanting, Inspector," he said. "Silence, yes? And what am I wanting as my price for same? It is very simple. You see, just only some weeks back a very, very good friend of mine was suddenly dying, a man who was a colleague to you, Inspector, though not of such high rank. A clerk only, but so much a friend to me that he was sometimes telling me one or two things I was wanting to know, yes?"

So that is who it was, Ghote thought, light flooding in. The informant we all suspected to be there. And that is why not so long ago we were nearly nabbing this damn kingpin in that raid on the beer bar. His informant had died.

He had known the man quite well, a good old, fat-bellied constable, three long-service stripes on his arm, who had managed to squeeze himself at last into an easy job as a clerk at headquarters. A nice fellow, if somewhat heavy-going. A family man. Too much inclined sometimes to lay down the law, to shake his head over "the modern generation."

And all along he had been the informant, the goinda, supplying Mama Chiplunkar with his tip-offs. And, yes, he had fallen dead one day as he had plodded about filing documents, misfiling a good many of them, too. The sudden event had caused a lot of talk, and no little commiseration. And all the time . . .

Then, riding on that thought like an evil arrows-shooting demon on a shambling, knock-kneed horse, came the realization of what Mama Chiplunkar must want as his price now. Quite simply he himself was expected to take over from that fat, old clerk-constable.

"No," he burst out. "No, no. I cannot do it. I will not do it."

Mama Chiplunkar just grinned.

"Yes, yes," he said. "That was what they told me you would say. But, come, think only. A small matter of business. I have something you are wanting, you have something I am wanting. It is no more than that. This is how things are done, Inspector."

He leaned forward earnestly.

"When I was a young man," he said, "coming from my village in the Konkan to Bombay itself and working-working in the docks, carrying, sweating, paining, sometimes a little-little smuggling, yes, or helping some crate only to smash and picking up one or two of whatsoever was inside, one day I was suddenly understanding about the way business must be done. Let me tell you how it was."

He paused and took another easy look up and down the road.

"Politician was coming down to docks," he continued, still smiling. "Election on way. I had what he was wanting. One vote. He was offering-offering what he was thinking I was wanting, rise in pay-rate, tomorrow. But by then I had learned I was wanting something more than just only promise. I was wanting rupees in the hand. And that I was telling him, and that I was getting because I was able to give him more of votes than just only mine. How? you are asking. I will tell. I could give him votes one hundred, two hundred, because those fellows were wanting what I had to give. No broken bones, yes? No heads banged up and down on stones of dockside, bang, bang, bang, yes? So I was making nice-nice deal. With them, with that politician. His name you are knowing, I am sure, but I am not saying, yes?"

Ghote thought he almost certainly did know the name, and the method. But he was not going to yield his assent to Mama Chiplunkar's greasy plea. At least he could preserve that much dignity.

"Come—" he began sharply.

But the gang boss was in too full a flow to be halted.

"Inspector," he went on, voice all honey, "ever since that day in docks I have known how this world is running. It is just only this: I have something somebody is wanting, he has something I am wanting. We do a deal."

"No!" Ghote burst out at last. "No. You are trying to make your shamelessness into something that is deserving of respect and admiration. But it is not so. No."

Mama Chiplunkar's head wagged in gentle negation.

"But it is, Inspectorji, it is. Look, how else was I myself rising up from dock laborer to famous social worker, houses and flats two-three, cars also? So let the two of us, you and I, just only make our deal, make it and shake hands."

"Shake hands with you? You blackmailer. You—you snake. Never. I will never do it."

The grin, big paan-stained teeth glinting, did not leave Mama Chiplunkar's round face for an instant.

"Well, if you are not wanting to shake-shake," he said, "I am not at all minding. So long as deal is done."

"Never."

The gang kingpin gave a fat chuckle.

"Well, perhaps tomorrow. I am not in so much of hurry. Tomorrow I would be here at this time only. And then we agree, hands shaking or not hands shaking."

He turned away. Some hundred yards farther along the road a gleaming black Ambassador, which Ghote had not till now realized was one of the kingpin's cars, began moving smoothly forward.

Mama Chiplunkar gave a quick glance back as he waddled toward it.

"And I would throw in one new scooter also," he called.

Bitterly Ghote stooped to heave up his old, unreliable machine from the side of the road where it had lain all the time he and the gang boss had been talking. Wearily, because he could think of nothing else to do, he put himself astride it and gave a kick to the starter lever. The motor fired at once.

He got little work done that morning. He ought, he knew, to be out and about once more attempting to track down that hanger-on of Mama Chiplunkar's the Assistant Commissioner believed might be the single drop that added to others would make eventually a milestone.

But what would be the good, he thought. If I am finding him only and if we are getting out of him some good information about where we could catch Chiplunkar red-handed with brown sugar on him, then it will be up to me to warn the man himself. And if I am not doing it, he will be taking that damn Ranchod and forcing him to make a full statement. Then it will be Arjun Singh or some other Vigilance Branch fellow coming to interview me, and going after to Dr. Commissariat.

He could not allow that to happen. For himself, though it would be the end of everything he had ever seen as his purpose in life, it would be bearable or something that had to be borne. If disaster struck, it struck. But Dr. Commissariat was another matter altogether. If Dr. Commissariat was arrested as Dolly Daruwala's murderer, a good man would be shown up before one and all as a sham and a hypocrite. His work for all the millions of India's downtrodden would almost certainly be lost. Whatever was good would be made into a laughingstock.

No, it must not be. It must not.

But how to avoid it? How?

Hours passed. Several times he was aware that his peon had come into the office, looked at him anxiously, and had gone out again. Twice the fellow had contrived to have some papers to put down in the desk tray at his elbow. But he scarcely saw him. A cup of tea had arrived on the desk, too, at some time. Had he paid the boy? He did not know.

At some point in the afternoon, he succeeded at last in stirring himself. He had, he forced himself to remember, until next morning before he had to decide. However much that decision, whichever way it went, was going to be only the first step on a path plunging and plunging downward.

In the compound outside his cabin he stood, heedless of the sun, and made himself think where it was he had got to the day before in his search for Mama Chiplunkar's wretched hanger-on. At last he succeeded in bringing back to his consciousness what seemed a pale, dreamlike sequence of events, his activities of the day before. And, yes, the next place he had decided to go to was a drinking den, the Beauty Bar.

Then at once he found himself thinking again what did it matter whether his inquiries there led to the fellow or not? When success could only mean the beginning of disaster.

But he set off nevertheless. There seemed to be nothing else to do but to carry on with his duties. But halfway to the bar, which was tucked away deep inside a building in Nagandas Master Road crammed with the offices of dozens of little businesses, he stopped and stood where he was on the pavement, heedless of hurrying Bombayites brushing past. Was there, he had found himself wondering, anyone at all he could confide in about the dilemma that stared at him. Protima? From her he would get sympathy, all the sympathy he could possibly want. But what good would sympathy do? What he wanted was a way out. And there was no way out.

Nor could he possibly tell his secret to any one of his

colleagues. That would be to put the weight and burden onto their shoulders also. Whether whoever he told advised him to defy Mama Chiplunkar or urged him to feed the crime kingpin with the tip-offs he was wanting made no difference. The only result would be that they, too, would be caught in the same iron trap as his own moment of decision lying underneath Dolly Daruwala's shiny green-covered bed had eventually clamped on to him.

And that had been, he thought with tears springing to his eyes, by the smallest of chances only. If on the evening Mr. Mistry had unexpectedly given Ranchod leave so that the fellow would not know Burjor Pipewalla was visiting Marzban Apartments, if then Ranchod, that card player, had decided to go somewhere for a game . . . or if he had only happened to stay asleep curled up in the darkness of the stairs when Dr. Commissariat had gone clattering past . . . then none of this would have happened. Or, again, if he himself had not made that one small slip when he had first gone to report to Mr. Mistry and had announced himself stupidly as "Inspector Ghote," then Ranchod would never have known who was the man he had seen coming down those dark stairs some minutes after Dr. Commissariat had woken him. Then he would have had nothing to exercise his petty piece of blackmail over. And in that case Mama Chiplunkar would never have learned the secret and seen how he could make use of it.

But no use blaming chance for always being on the wrong side, no use imagining what had never happened. The fact was that two terrible alternatives faced him, and he had to accept one or the other.

He had to defy Mama Chiplunkar and before long find himself dismissed in ignominy from the service that was the whole point and purpose of his working life, and with that see that truly good man Dr. Commissariat led like a common thief to the cells. Or he had to stick it out and every hour be ready to betray all he had believed in since the day he had joined service as a probationary subinspector.

For a moment the hopelessness of it all made him contemplate the only other way of escape open to him, escape altogether from

a life that seemed to be nothing but his two impossible alternatives. But he knew he could not take that way. Some spark lay
deep within him that he did not have the power to tread out. It
was hardly the thought of how suicide would be failing Protima
and, as bad or worse, somehow failing the promise that was
young Ved, the hope lying in his wanting that talisman of the
future, the home computer. That weighed with him, as did his
feeling for his duty to the service. But what, he knew, made this
final escape impossible was simply that nothing, not even Mama
Chiplunkar's unchallengeable arguments, could quite kill in him
hope.

But what hope he had he could not in any way make out.

The secret that Ranchod had by chance acquired had been
learned by Mama Chiplunkar, a man who knew its full worth. A
man who, simply and without anything but the merest skin of
pretense, was prepared to use it to make a deal. And there was
nothing to be done.

He was caught. Caught. And tomorrow, early in the morning,
he would have to pay one of the prices Mama Chiplunkar had
demanded. Disgrace, or behavior meriting every disgrace he
could heap upon himself.

He forced himself back to the present, stumped up to the
Beauty Bar, saw that his quarry was not there.

So much the better. So much the worse.

THIRTEEN

Ghote's scooter started at first try next morning. He cursed it.

He had felt obliged to leave home in particularly good time so as to be outside when Mama Chiplunkar appeared, as he had no doubt the business-blackmailer would. He had expected to be found, as he had been the day before, kicking and kicking at the scooter's starting lever. But now he was left, standing beside the wretched machine, obliged to listen to it throbbing so noisily that whatever the two of them had to say would be in danger of being altogether drowned out.

Not that he knew what he himself was going to say. He had spent the night dozing and waking, turning and tossing, thankful only that Protima seemed to be sleeping particularly well. She had the knack of asking the very questions he most wished not to answer. The evening before, too, he had taken pains to keep away from her, telephoning briefly from headquarters to say a case was keeping him. But not all his heart-searchings of the night, and his equally tense mental arguments at his desk in the evening as he had made efforts to deal with his paperwork, had got him any nearer to finding an answer to give the brown-sugar kingpin.

The fact of the matter was, he knew, that there was no answer.

But now in the quiet of the early morning—here and there along the road people were still lying on the pavement asleep—

he saw Mama Chiplunkar's black Ambassador turn the corner. In a moment it drew up, some hundred yards from where he was standing beside his still rhythmically shaking machine. Mama Chiplunkar got out, gave some order to his driver, and advanced down the road.

What was he going to say to him? He knew no more now than when he had watched him go the morning before, and had then unexpectedly kicked his scooter into instant life.

"Good morning, Inspector. Tell me, you are in better mood today? You are ready to do business-business, yes?"

Ghote muttered a yes. What else can I say, he thought.

"Good, good. So you are agreeing?"

Now is the moment I must do it: the fearful signal flashed up in Ghote's mind. No more of shilly-shally. It is now or never. Some answer I must give. Now. Now, it is either "Go to hell," or it is "Very well, Chiplunkar sahib, you are giving me no alternative."

"Very well, Chiplunkar sahib, you are giving me no alternative."

He felt as if it had not been himself who had pronounced the words, and pronounce them loudly he had over the explosive throbbing of his scooter. But said they had been, if by some other-Ghote standing there in his clean gray cotton trousers and the red-and-blue-checked shirt Protima had ironed for him the evening before. The words had been said. The choice had been made.

"And now you will shake, Inspector?"

For a moment Ghote was almost prepared to submit to this last act of humiliation. He felt he had already lost so much. He might as well lose whatever remaining shreds of pride he had left in the profession he had wanted to be part of from his earliest boyhood and had taken in from the day he had first reported for duty at police training school.

But then some tiny warning instinct buzzed in his head. He glanced back toward Mama Chiplunkar's car. Yes, it looked as though the driver might well be watching whatever it was his boss was doing. There would be a witness to this agreement between a police inspector and a crime kingpin. And he was now someone who had to guard against any one of his secret actions being observed by any witness whatsoever.

"No," he said. "No handshakes. I have agreed. That must be enough."

"As you are liking, Inspector, as you are liking. Just only so long as you are giving me good warnings when I am needing same. Remember, I am looking to you to be always finding out what is happening against me. And, ek dum, when you are finding you must let me know."

He gave a quick look this way and that along the road.

"Now," he went on, "I am going to give you one telephone number. It is secret-secret. So soon as you have anything to tell, ring at once 4520775. If I am not there, someone I am altogether trusting would be. Night and day also. So ring. I will say that number once again. It is 4520775. Now, you have by-hearted it?"

"Yes," Ghote said. "It is 4520775. I would not forget."

He felt somehow as if that string of figures, which already he knew he would not be able to force from his mind, however little he wished to have it there, was a stamped seal. A seal set on his treachery.

This was the day when he had to put together the papers for Shiv Chand's appearance at the Court of Sessions on the charge under Section 383 of the Indian Penal Code, extortion. He congratulated himself dully that the task had come when it had. If he was in his seat all day, working through statements, checking and rechecking, making sure his two panches—the old Parsi, Mr. Framrose, and the timid young municipal building inspector—were ready, then he was altogether unlikely to catch any gossip about the operation against Mama Chiplunkar. He would have nothing he ought, if he was to keep his bargain, to pass on.

But he knew that this was a respite only, and the shortest of respites. Next day he would in the ordinary course of events be spending less time behind the closed bat-wing doors that kept out any of his colleagues without some particular need to see him. Then he would have to force himself to go about taking the active steps on Mama Chiplunkar's behalf that the gang kingpin would expect of him. If he failed to warn him of some planned raid and he was caught in it, the first thing he would do would be to take revenge on a blackmail victim who had defied him. He would produce from wherever it was he was keeping Ranchod captive this witness that a Crime Branch officer had let a murderer go free. Giving Vigilance Branch that name would be a powerful counter in his efforts to get himself out of trouble.

The Shiv Chand paperwork, however, was not so absorbing that from time to time he found he was ceasing to pay it attention. Instead his mind kept going back and back to that first early-morning meeting with Mama Chiplunkar. Should he have acted differently then? Should he simply have come out at once on the spot with the Duke Wellington answer?

Was it even now too late? Could he not go to the Assistant Commissioner at this moment and tell him exactly what Mama Chiplunkar had attempted to do? There would be no need to say that, for some few hours, he actually had cowed down to the man's blackmail. If that came out later, he could deny it to one hundred percent. It would be his word only against that of a known criminal.

But, no, going to the Assistant Commissioner would mean telling him exactly what Mama Chiplunkar knew that he had used to blackmail him. And that would betray Dr. Commissariat.

No, he had been faced with two alternatives, each as appalling as the other. And, for better or worse, he had chosen the one that he had.

He hardly, even now, knew why he had made that choice. Perhaps, he thought, putting out a feeble, waving tentacle toward some shadow of a steady rock, it had been the alternative that gave out some hope. At least it meant that disaster would not strike at once. Perhaps something would somehow . . . While, if he had done what he had truly wanted to do and said, "Be publishing and be damned," then already today perhaps Arjun Singh or someone else from Vigilance would be barging through his door demanding answers.

He came at last to the end of the day. All the papers necessary for Shiv Chand's trial were ready to the last dotted *i*, the last crossed *t*.

And, he reflected, I have done the work damn well. No one would be finding one mistake—when they come to take over from an officer suspended in disgrace, suspended if not for having allowed a murderer to go scot-free then for having given information to a known criminal.

He left headquarters almost like a fugitive. He cursed and cursed at his scooter when, once again, it failed to start at first kick. And when he did get it to go, he rode toward the gate with guilty looks left and right all the way in case some colleague newly allocated a task in the operation against Chiplunkar should stop him wanting to chat.

But at least, he thought, as at last he shot out of the gate with the machine spluttering and jerking beneath him, at least I have resisted taking the bribe of a new scooter. And if Mama Chiplunkar had offered again after I had agreed to his stinking plan, then I would have given him the selfsame answer as before. At least there is that.

But one day's grace was only one day's grace, and it was with that thought swirling darkly in his mind that he arrived home. For a moment, standing with his hand raised to tap the outer latch, he actually peered into the dark corner where Ranchod had been accustomed to stand on his regular monthly visits. How good it would be if the man was there again, slobbering and squinting, hand held out demanding. Just only to have to pay him his hundred rupees and be done with it. That regular transaction had truly seemed almost a pleasure. It had been a visible sign that he was continuing to do what he had undertaken to at that moment when he had deliberately stayed hidden under Dolly Daruwala's bed with her murderer not two feet away from him. It had been the confirmation of his decision to protect a truly good man. A man of positive good, even with that good taking the form of killing a fellow human being. That human being had, indisputably, been a vermin, pest, and snake. The good man had done what was right, never mind the sections and subsections of the Indian Penal Code.

Yes, there had been a sort of comfort in being blackmailed by Ranchod.

But there was no pleasure at all in being under the thumb of business-business Mama Chiplunkar.

With an effort of will that brought a film of sweat to his forehead he tapped at his own door, behind which lay the reality of having to keep stone-buried within himself the dilemma his protecting Dr. Commissariat had now created for him.

But no amount of willed effort could help him, once inside, to behave with anything of his customary ease. He could bring himself to do no more than give the tersest of answers to anything Protima or Ved said. And when he realized that Protima had judged his state so well that she was refraining, if with difficulty, from asking him the reason, it served only to make him more rebelliously determined to sit in silence.

But eventually it was borne in on him that Ved was hovering around instead of quietly getting on with his studies. For some time, however, his black depression prevented him recalling Ved's stratagem with the newspaper cutting. Then he remembered. So, the boy must know now it had been successful. Or successful at least to the extent of the existence of a secondhand home computer being drawn to his own attention.

What had he said in response when Protima had made him look at the cutting? He could not remember. All that business seemed to have taken place in some far distant time, in another world. But he had certainly not agreed outright to getting the computer. Yet neither—so his groping mind told him—had he come out with a total refusal.

He must have said something that would have given Protima reason to believe he was capable of being won around. And she would have passed on the news. Probably she had been telling it to the boy at just the time Mama Chiplunkar had made that first approach. There must be, too, he gradually got himself around to thinking, a certain urgency about the matter. At any moment, really, some other bright boy from anywhere in Bombay might have persuaded a father to get together the money to buy at such a bargain price this key to a golden future.

And plainly, now he looked at Ved, the boy was filled with anxiety. He wanted an answer. A decision to buy or not to, which he himself should have made well before this, meant everything to him.

So would it not be best just to lift up his head now and say he could reply to the advertisement and that, somehow, the money would be there?

But he could not do it. He knew that he ought to. Or that he ought to bring himself to say that the sum required was really too much to find. But bowed beneath the weight that Mama Chiplunkar had placed crushingly on him, he lacked the will.

For one viciously ironic instant he even said to himself that he would only have to ring that number, 4520775—no, he had not been able to get it out of his head—and demand as an extra for his services the three thousand rupees the home computer cost and he would get it. But the moment passed almost before it had arrived. No, he would never take one paisa from that man.

But that did not mean that he was not utterly under his thumb.

Yet thicker billows of depression rolled through him.

He was deprived even of the energy to push himself up from his chair and pretend he needed an early night. So he sat on, silent and glowering, till first Protima sent a plainly disconsolate Ved off to bed, and then she herself said that if he was going to go on sitting she at least was tired out and was not going to wait. And still he stayed slumped where he was, and it was well past midnight before at last he found enough strength of mind to stagger to his feet and take himself off.

Nor at headquarters next day was he able, as he had foreseen, to hide in the slight sanctuary of his office. As duties took him here and there about the compound he knew at every step what he ought to be doing. If he was not to risk Mama Chiplunkar revengefully betraying his secret, he ought to hail any colleague he saw and casually bring into the conversation the operation against the brown-sugar kingpin. There would be no difficulty in doing so, either. The operation was engaging almost every man in Crime Branch and there would be gossip and guessing in plenty about what was planned next.

But, though he had more than one opportunity, every time he balked at the last moment. Yet in the end, unexpectedly, a chance arose that he felt he could not fail to take. It happened when he found himself standing at a urinal stall in the mutri next to a visitor to headquarters, the bandmaster of the police band. He knew him just to speak to, a surly fellow who believed that the whole of the Bombay Police existed simply so that his band could play its music.

"Well, Inspector," the old fellow said in answer to the word of greeting he had felt bound to offer him, "is it that you also are busy with this burra Chiplunkar bandobast? You know I am here because they are talking of taking my fellows from their duties? I was telling Commissioner himself my men have more important things to be doing than running after some brown-sugar badmash."

Then he knew the moment had come. For the first time in his life he had to attempt to learn a secret in order to pass it on to a criminal.

He swallowed hard.

"So, Bandmaster sahib," he said, dry-mouthed, "Commissioner is planning some big raid somewhere?"

"No, no. Not yet. And if you are asking me, he is not at all knowing when to raid or where. Whole damn thing is getting nowhere, I am believing. It is nothing but one whim of Commissioner's. One whim only."

Ghote felt the words as a shower of cooling rain in the days of premonsoon oppressiveness. So nothing was planned. Or nothing for the immediate future. For some time to come at least he could be the goinda at headquarters without betraying his lifelong trust. Or he could do so if what his sour old acquaintance had said was the truth. And in the meanwhile something might happen. Something . . .

He walked out of the mutri feeling suddenly almost happy. And in any case, he thought, tomorrow I am giving evidence in

the Shiv Chand trial and there will be no chance of hearing office
gup in the Court of Sessions.

So he sailed into headquarters next day—the evening at home
had gone better, and he had even managed to say he was still
considering the home computer advertisement—with the feeling
that all might not be totally lost, however little he could see any
way of getting out from under Mama Chiplunkar's blackmail. At
once his telephone jangled and, picking up the receiver, he heard
the Assistant Commissioner's voice.

"Ghote? Come up, will you?"

"Yes, sir. Straightaway, sir."

What could the A.C.P. want? He must know from the big
duties board behind his desk that this was the day he himself was
in court. There could be no question of orders for him.

He hurried up to the A.C.P.'s big cabin, peered through the
square window in the door to see whether the A.C.P. was
engaged, found that he was not, knocked, and entered.

"You sent for me, sir?"

"Yes. Yes, Ghote. This Shiv Chand trial . . . that the fellow's
name?"

"Yes, sir. Yes."

"Lot of interest in it. Interest in certain circles. Now, I want
you to make sure there won't be anything in your evidence that
is going to cause—to cause unpleasantness connected with that
book *Indians of Distinction and Merit.*"

"*Indians of Merit and Distinction,* sir," Ghote corrected auto-
matically, busy thinking whether, although the only charge
against Freddy Kersasp's former office manager was of attempting to extort money from the pianist Falli Bamboat, some
mention of other entries in the always-unprinted volume might
not arise.

"Well, man?"

"No, sir. No, there is the one charge only and that is
concerning the man himself and no other."

"Good, good. Damn nuisance all this just when the operation
against Chiplunkar is coming to the climax. We've known all
about that laboratory at Multiplex Chemicals and Drug Manu-

facturing for weeks, of course, but now, just when I am ready to give the green signal to catch the fellow there red-handed, I get these damned inquiries about that appalling *Gup Shup*. I must say I thought I'd heard the last of that rag weeks ago."

Ghote felt as if a sudden huge iron collar had been placed round his neck. To learn this now, now when he had believed himself off the hook at least for a few hours. To have full details of an operation against Mama Chiplunkar thrust at him. To be told exactly what the brown-sugar kingpin would most need to know. It was wrong. It was unfair. It should never have happened.

"Right then, Inspector. That's all I was wanting. Thank you."

"Sir."

Ghote watched himself, as if from a distant cinema seat, click heels in salute and turn to go. And then he heard the Assistant Commissioner's voice again, coming from as far away.

"Oh, and keep all that under your hat, Ghote, won't you? Security involved. Only a handful of people in the know as yet."

"Yes, sir. Yes."

Should he walk, walk like a mechanical man, straight out of the compound to the nearest safe telephone and ring 4520775 at once? That was the bargain with Chiplunkar.

But he could not do it. Not yet. Not quite yet.

He went down, almost staggering, to his office and groped his way to his chair.

Think. He had to think.

He looked at his watch and at last made out what time its hands were saying. He had only half an hour at the most before he was due to leave for court.

Mentally he composed the message of warning he did not know how he could avoid giving Mama Chiplunkar. "They are knowing about Multiplex Chemicals and Drug Manufacturing. They are waiting till you come there, Chiplunkar sahib, and then they are ready to raid." That would be enough.

It would be too much. It would be the act of treachery finally and fully committed.

No, he could not do it. He could not. But how to avoid it? To

go back up to the Assistant Commissioner, insist on seeing him
again and confess all? But that would be to commit his act of
treachery against Dr. Commissariat. It would be worse. Worse.
   He sat there stultified.

   And then, with strong in his mind the unforgotten sight of the
Parsi scientist standing above the body of Dolly Daruwala,
the thin shining steel blade of his gupti protruding from the
rose-pink sari covering her plump frame, a thought came to him.
A thought as terrible, in its way, as that of betraying Dr.
Commissariat, as that of betraying his duty as a police officer.

   There was, after all, one other way to take. One other way out
of his iron-bound dilemma. He could himself eliminate Mama
Chiplunkar as a vermin, snake, and pest. He could kill the fellow.

FOURTEEN

It needed an effort of will that gave him a feeling of nausea strong enough to make him sway in his chair for Ghote to get up, collect together what he needed, and go and shepherd his two waiting panches to the Court of Sessions. Had he loosened his grip on himself for an instant, he felt, he would have collapsed back into the chair and sat there hour after hour, heedless of his duty in court, thinking of nothing but the decision that had come to him. The decision he had taken.

At least, he thought, he had spared himself the need to go, or not to go, to a telephone and call that number 4520775 to give Mama Chiplunkar his warning. If the man had not long to live, it did not in any way matter whether he was warned of his danger or not. For now all he had to do was to make sure his part in Shiv Chand's trial went without hitch. While the trial lasted—and he did not expect a clear case like Shiv Chand's to take long—he would not need to think. Thinking would have to come, the working out of how to do what he had decided must be done. But it need not be yet.

Most of the proceedings in court passed by him as if they were happening in another city, in another country. He was conscious that both his panches gave their evidence without any complications. The young municipal building inspector had looked terribly gray, but he had stumbled through. Mr. Framrose was much better, dignified, concise, and evidently trustworthy. His own evidence he produced without hesitation or lapse. But beyond that, and at the end registering that Shiv Chand had duly been found guilty and sentenced to one year's rigorous imprisonment, nothing impinged.

Still moving like an automaton, he returned to headquarters and hurried into his office.

The moment he sat himself in the chair where, some three hours earlier, he had made his fearful decision, it all came back to him. It was as if a switch had been pressed and letters had appeared on a screen. *I must kill Mama Chiplunkar.*

At once his mind started busily working out details. He was not going to go bald-headed to the man and strangle him with his bare hands. No, this needed the same deliberate planning as Dr. Commissariat had shown in disposing of Dolly Daruwala. It needed, however soon it must be done, the equivalent of Dr. Commissariat's briefcase full of currency notes that, handed over, had induced Dolly Daruwala to open her safe so that all the evidence it contained could be destroyed. It needed similar forethought to Dr. Commissariat's acquisition of a gupti, and its use over a period as a simple walking cane so that arriving in the flat with it would arouse no suspicion till the sword inside was drawn. It needed taking precautions as careful as Dr. Commissariat's in touching nothing during the whole time he had been at the scene.

But where was the scene of Mama Chiplunkar's disposal to be? He had to find somewhere isolated, lonely. But where in crowded, people-crammed Bombay could he do that? The old European cemetery at Sewri? No, beggars and the homeless were to be found at every hour among its moldering tombs. Out among the salt flats? It might be deserted enough somewhere there, but on what possible pretext could he induce Mama Chiplunkar to meet him at such a place? None. Plainly none.

An idea came to him. There was something better than a deserted place. A crowded place. Somewhere where among thousands of people all unknown to one another he and Mama

Chiplunkar would be virtually on their own. And the moment the thought had come he found he knew exactly the place. A suburban-line railway station. One where people in their hundreds waited each evening in striving, struggling, jam-packed masses for trains to take them home. It would be easy there, surely, simply to give his victim one sharp push as a train approached, and then to melt into the throng of determined passengers waiting for the next one and slip away. It would be necessary, of course, to take some precautions. To wear inconspicuous clothing, to look around and guard against the almost impossible coincidence of someone who knew him by sight being at—where precisely? Why, at Grant Road station. This very evening. In the rush hour. That would do it. It was almost made for it.

Abruptly he looked up, caught a glimpse of his face in the little square of mirror hanging on the far wall.

What was he doing? he asked himself in sudden panic. What was he saying to himself? What, in God's name, was he planning? He was planning—he licked his dry lips—he was planning to kill someone. To murder them. To commit murder. Yes, very well, the man he had in mind was at the far end of the scale of wickedness, a top distributor of that vile, death-dealing drug, brown sugar. He was a blackmailer, too. One perfectly prepared to use a fact he had come across almost by chance to force a police officer to betray his trust, to aid and assist him in evading the rightful forces of the law. But that man was still a human being, one who had some claim to life unless and until the law, in all its majesty, with all its care, decided that he was no longer fit to live.

He sat for a while breathing heavily, his mind emptied again of every thought as if it had been violently pumped dry.

Then, slowly, the facts he had considered before he had set off for the Court of Sessions began to come, step by logical step, back to him. Yes, Mama Chiplunkar had him locked in an impossible dilemma. There was no way out of it. Either he went to a telephone even now and passed on the strictly secret information he had happened to learn, or he did not. And if he sat tight until Mama Chiplunkar had gone to this Multiplex factory, where opium was being turned into crude heroin, and had been caught there, that would mean—there could be no doubting it—squinting Ranchod would be taken around to Vigilance Branch to betray him. In absolute consequence then, that man of goodness, Dr. Commissariat, would be betrayed in his turn. To break that stranglehold there was only one thing to be done. Mama Chiplunkar had to killed.

Yes, the decision, really, was taken. It had been taken from the moment the possibility of it had entered his head. The man must die. That he himself was to carry out the deed was, somehow, only a minor consideration. It was to be. It was there. There was nothing else to be said.

But how to get Mama Chiplunkar to the chosen place and at the right time? As quickly as he had asked himself the question the answer appeared, as if the whole plan had been stored up waiting for him. He had been given the very instrument, so to speak. That emergency warning telephone number, 4520775. He had, after all, only to ring Mama Chiplunkar there and say that "they" had learned about the Multiplex Chemicals and Drug Manufacturing place probably from someone in his gang itself, but that so far he had not been able to find out the man's name though he should have it by the evening. Mama Chiplunkar might then even suggest himself that they should meet, and he could quickly give him his chosen time and place and at once end the call. Yes, that should do it. It would need a little chalak, but he ought to be able to manage it.

Without hesitation he got up and left. There was a telephone he could use safe from being overheard at the paanwalla's stall not three minutes away.

Would Mama Chiplunkar come? Ghote prowled up and down a short stretch of the platform at Grant Road station, weaving his way mechanically through the dense collection of Bombayites leaving offices and shops to make their way to the far-off suburbs. Clerks in limp, sweat-patched shirts, secretaries in cheap cotton saris clutching plastic shopping baskets, a cluster of Goan girls in

blouses and skirts chattering together in English laced with the
last traces of Portuguese. Pushing their way through the tired
waiting mass went vendors of this and that, a boy with evening
papers hooked in a huge bundle under a string-thin arm, a
hawker of jasmine garlands, their sweet scent made rank at this
late hour of the day, a kelawalli, her last few sad-looking bananas
sulking at the bottom of the round wide basket she had lifted
exhaustedly from her head.

His telephone call to the brown-sugar kingpin had gone every
bit as well as he could have expected. He had got straight on to
the man himself, and had contrived to bang down the receiver
the moment he had pushed out the place and time for this
meeting.

As he had dropped the coins for the call onto the paanwalla's
gleaming brass tray, he had thought to himself with strangely
savored irony that, by passing on the very warning about the
observation mounted at Multiplex Chemicals and Drug Manufacturing, he had in fact done what earlier he had wished with his
whole being he would never have to do. But the beauty of it was
that it no longer mattered. Because sentence of death had been
passed on Mama Chiplunkar. The fellow would not live to
benefit by what he believed he had extracted with such calm
insistence from the helpless victim of his blackmail.

The exact spot he had rapidly said to Mama Chiplunkar that he
would wait at was on the platform for trains leaving the city, at
the end nearest the terminus. It was the very best place for what
he had undertaken to do. Any incoming train would still be
going at speed at this point. One quick push at the right moment
and it would be over. All that was necessary was to get Mama
Chiplunkar near enough to the edge of the platform. If he could
contrive to move in that direction as they talked it would be done
in a second.

With a twice-repeated poop-poop a train approached, as at this
hour of the evening they did at three- or four-minute intervals.
He watched it slacken in speed and come to a noisy halt. The
waiting crowd on the platform surged forward toward the
ever-open doors. Somehow the pressure squeezed the already

packed passengers inside back a little, and at each set of doors some dozen people managed to force themselves in, as determined at the ladies-only compartments as at any of the others. Above the jammed, sweating masses inside, the train's fans twirled ineffectually.

The guard blew his whistle, the sound shrill above the general hubbub, and swung himself on board. Slowly the train began to move off. The unsuccessful would-be passengers reluctantly fell back. Here and there in the long length of the platform a daring young man leaped forward at the last instant and clung precariously to whatever hold he could find on the ever more swiftly moving train, swinging far out over the platform edge and then over the track. Shuddering and screamingly rattling, the steel monster at last disappeared from view.

And, yes, Ghote thought, the next one, or the one after that, or the one after that again, would be the one. If only Mama Chiplunkar would come.

He looked at his watch. In theory the fellow was still not late. There were three, perhaps four, minutes before the hour he had proposed.

He forced himself to take one more stroll along the platform. It would occupy the time, and it would make him less conspicuous than if he were to stand at his chosen spot consulting his watch every ten or fifteen seconds. He set off, weaving his way through the crowd where it was thinnest at the farthest point from the platform edge. Idly he made a show of looking at the posters on the wall beside him. BEFORE YOU BUY A CHEAP AIR CONDITIONER—SOME CHILLING TRUTHS. Well, AC had never been within his means. I WAS IMPRESSED WHEN MY DOCTOR SAID KEO-KARPIN HAIR VITALIZER REALLY STOPS HAIR LOSS.

He found he was unable to refrain from passing a hand over his own head, though "hair loss" was not one of his troubles.

But what it is they are doing? he thought abruptly. They are blackmailing me or anybody who has lost a few only hairs. Yes, that is what it is. Blackmail. And that goes for the A-C also. They are blackmailing anybody who has paid the minimum by stating, without actually saying it, that any cheap machine will conk out.

Blackmail, blackmail, blackmail. Not as altogether bad as Mama Chiplunkar's, or even as Freddy Kersasp and his *Gup Shup*, but still blackmail.

He looked to see if all the other posters were as unpleasantly persuasive.

PRESTIGE—COME BY IT NATURALLY WITH RAYMOND'S SUITINGS, SHIRTINGS, TROUSERINGS. Yes, that was attempting to obtain money from the innocent by making them feel they were altogether lacking in "prestige." Then there was that big ad for cigarettes with the picture of the handsome boy and the seductive, modern-looking girl. MADE FOR EACH OTHER. Yes, what was that saying but "If you are not smoking our cigarettes you will not be one successful lover"? Blackmail. Blackmail, again. And those small-small letters underneath: CIGARETTE SMOKING IS INJURIOUS TO HEALTH. They did nothing to take away from the message. And was not that blackmail also? Even if it was blackmail to good purpose, as his own blackmailing of Freddy Kersasp had been. Perhaps.

Now, abruptly, he looked at his watch once more. Okay. He had not let too much time slip by, entwined in that sudden quagmire-revealing vision.

He turned back toward his chosen spot.

In his mind he felt the whole procedure he was to go through as being fixedly laid down. It was a pattern already embarked upon to be simply followed to its end. Mama Chiplunkar was a vermin, snake, and pest who by the foulest of means had maneuvered himself into a position where he could guarantee himself immunity from the servants of justice. He deserved to be eliminated. He would be. And by the very instrument the man himself had selected. He would be eliminated at the hands of a person he believed unable to do anything other than what he had demanded. It was just.

Lost in these thoughts he banged up against a tea-boy coming from the stall farther along the platform, six glasses in his wire basket. All but two of them slopped out the best part of their contents.

At once the boy—he could not have been more than twelve—launched into a splatter of abuse in the foulest Marathi.

"Take them back to the stall," Ghote said, overcome by remorse all the sharper for what he had been thinking when the accident had occurred. "I will pay for them to be filled again."

He noticed, with a gleam of amusement he was surprised to find himself capable of now, that the urchin was taking pains to place himself where he could make sure this unusually accommodating person was not planning some trick. Together they approached the tea stall, its front bright with a giant painted cup on a glaring blue background, a thick black wisp of steam twisting upward from it. Above, the rate list in crude red lettering in Hindi and English offered TEA—COFFEE—JAM CAKE—SAMOSA. Ghote planked some coins on the counter next to the shiny tea urn and moved away at once.

What if, while his back had been turned, Mama Chiplunkar had come? Had taken a careful look and, because he himself was not at the exact place specified, had decided this was some police trap? Had immediately made off?

But, no.

There standing at the very spot, looking around comfortably and without hurry, was the plump, white-clad form.

Without hesitation Ghote went up to him.

"Chiplunkar sahib."

"Ah, it is you, Inspector. Good, good. Now what is it you have to tell? There is someone informing on me to you policewallas, yes?"

Ghote seized on the chance his victim had given him. With something to say that would hold his fullest attention he could easily drift him toward the edge of the platform. The deadly edge.

"I am very much fearing there is one goinda in your outfit, Chiplunkar sahib," he said.

The look of vicious intent he saw then in the gang boss's little fat-encased eyes confirmed for him, if more confirmation was at all needed, that here was a man of evil. A vermin. A snake. A pest.

And with a deadly sting, ready at the slightest crossing of his will to dart out poison.

But how to keep the talk going while not losing the intentness that was robbing the man of every other consideration?

He put on an expression of acute anxiety.

"Chiplunkar sahib," he said, "please understand, it is very difficult for me."

Chiplunkar's small mouth hardened into a short, uncompromising line.

"Difficult-difficult," he said. "I want none of that from you. From you I am wanting just only one name. Who it is? Who it is who has dared . . . ?"

Ghote swallowed, and not by any means in pretended apprehension. This man was deadly dangerous. No doubt about it. Compared to Mr. Z. R. Mistry's "most dangerous woman in Bombay," he was a cobra set against a mosquito.

He put on a show of looking all round as if he believed that even here one of Chiplunkar's toadies and hangers-on might be watching. That the goinda himself, sneaking after his boss, might be ready at this very last moment to prevent him discovering his name.

And he took two quick paces toward the edge of the platform.

Luckily at just the point he was making for there was a small gap in the line of would-be passengers waiting for the next train, the train due at any moment. The spot could look like somewhere where it would be safer to murmur a secret.

He felt a shiver of triumph as Chiplunkar without any hesitation stepped forward at his side.

If only a train would come in another instant, as soon as they both had taken two more steps forward. The circumstances were so precisely right. Although there was no one within two or three feet to either side of the spot he was aiming for, not far behind there were enough people for him to be able to step back sharply the moment he pushed Chiplunkar down in front of the onward-rushing blank steel monster. Then in a second he would be not the man standing beside the fellow who had fallen under the train, but simply one of the crowd of shocked onlookers.

Dressed as he was in his oldest shirt—the green one with the wavy black squares by happy chance kept in his office to change into after his court appearance in uniform—he would look altogether like any of the weary waiting clerks or shop salesmen lined up to his rear.

But above the noisy clamor all around, he could hear no sign of any new train approaching. The jabbering of the waiting passengers, the squealing of car brakes as rush-hour vehicles making their way along Naushir Barucha Marg parallel to the rail tracks halted, moved on, halted again, their incessant, irritated, and illegal hooting, with a little farther off the roar of buses, and everywhere the unending caw-caw-cawing of the crows, blotted out all more distant sounds. But surely a train must come soon. Surely.

In the meantime he must hold Chiplunkar's attention, come what may.

Rapidly through his mind he ran the names of such members of Chiplunkar's gang as he knew. But how safe would it be to point the finger at any one of them? The man with the name he chose might well, for some reason he could not even guess at, be impossible as the police spy. Already behind bars. Sent away days before on some distant errand. Long ago externed from the city and forced to obey the magistrate's order.

No, he must find something else to hold his man.

Already Chiplunkar was beginning to look around about him. Was he, after all, wondering now whether this secret meeting was being observed? Was he half suspecting a police trap? Had it just crossed his mind that this tool of his might, despite everything, have gone to the Assistant Commissioner? Have told him what he had done? And, to earn back something of his good name, might have agreed to lure the man they so much wanted to a place where he could be picked up without trouble?

But, no, the fellow could not possibly have ideas like that. He would know, if anybody did, that it was only of use to the police to arrest him with evidence of dealings in brown sugar on his person.

He risked one more casual step. And another.

And Chiplunkar, as if positively proving his lack of suspicion, came to stand beside him at the platform edge, pushed even closer to the drop by an old toy seller, a bundle of bright balloons, red, yellow, blue, green, floating above his worn gray head.

If only a train would come.

He cocked his head and strained to hear the familiar clattering onrush above the row all around. But he could make out nothing.

"Chiplunkar sahib," he said hastily, "as I was telling per telephone, we—they—the police are knowing about Multiplex Chemicals and Drug Manufacturing. Just where it is, just what is being done in the place. Everything is ready for when you are coming there."

"Yes, yes. You have done well by me there, Inspector, I am telling you. You are earning your price, just as I am paying mine by keeping that fellow Ranchod safely shut away for you. It is what I am saying, we are having a deal. Business-business."

Ghote endeavored to put on a look of doglike gratitude.

"That name, Inspector?" Chiplunkar shot out brutally. "That name I am wanting."

Ghote could only fight to keep from his features the mingled feelings of perplexity and something not far off fear that he was experiencing.

What could he say to the man now? What dare he say?

And then, with an altogether sudden rush of sound, he heard behind him the noise of a fast-approaching train.

He pretended, with a gesture, that the sound was already making it difficult to be heard.

Chiplunkar wagged his round head up and down once in acknowledgment and prepared to wait till the train had come to a stop. Behind them both Ghote could sense the waiting passengers nudging forward. Conditions were ideal.

He took a quarter step back, so as to be in a position to give the brown-sugar kingpin that short swift inconspicuous shove at just the judged moment. He turned—the movement was perfectly natural—to face the arriving train.

Its buff-yellow front was only thirty yards distant. Twenty. Ten. The noise it was making was overwhelming.

Now. It was now.

And he failed to do it. Some inner person, deeper buried even than the man he had believed he had found in himself who was prepared to kill, stopped him. A life had been in his hands. He could not, he was not in his deepest self able to take it.

FIFTEEN

The train under which Mama Chiplunkar had not perished came to a halt. From behind Ghote as he stood beside and a little to the rear of the crime kingpin at the platform's edge—the rush of air accompanying the speeding steel monster had buffeted his whole body—the waiting passengers surged forward. In a moment they were at the open door in front of them, pushing and shoving, squeezing and wriggling in passionate attempts to secure themselves room on board.

Ghote and Mama Chiplunkar stood there, knocked and scraped by the battering torrent. Plainly it was still hopeless to try to communicate.

And what must I say to him now? Ghote asked himself in something like horror. One minute ago I was promising to inform him of the name of a goinda for the police among his hangers-on. It did not matter then that I had invented that fellow. Chiplunkar was under sentence of death. Before he had heard one word of what I had seemed to promise to tell him he would have been a mangled corpse under the wheels of this train here, halted, now.

But instead he is standing beside me. Hale and hearty. And just only as soon as the train is given the green signal and is moving away, while those who did not succeed to get in are dropping back, he will expect me to give him that name. And, worse, worse, worse, already I have given him one true fact that I should never have let pass beyond my lips. I have told him that the police know of that laboratory making brown sugar, Multiplex Chemicals and Drug Manufacturing, and that they are waiting to nab him there.

What to do?

His mind was blank. All willpower seemed to have been drained from him. Dimly, as if from some other planet altogether, he heard a shrill blast of sound. The guard's whistle. At once the train in front of him began heavily to get into motion. The would-be passengers at his side stepped back in resignation.

And in a minute, in much less, in a few seconds only, Mama Chiplunkar would turn to him demanding to know who was the goinda in his gang, the totally false goinda.

Now the train was beginning to gather speed, once again creating too much noise to make words audible. But for only seconds more. Already the succession of its open doors was starting to blur into an intermittent pattern: people, train side, people, train side.

Then he did it. It came to him in an almost simultaneous conjunction of decision and action. He launched into a long-stepping run, took a wild leap forward, hand reaching for a hold, and swung himself into, or half into, one of the open doors rushing past.

The strain on his arm was fearful, as if some monster from prehistoric days was endeavoring to tear it off. But then his left foot found a firm grip on the carriage floor, and the strain miraculously eased.

He turned his head. Mama Chiplunkar was standing there where he had left him, mouth agape in astonishment.

"No!" he yelled back at him with all the force of his lungs. "No! No! No!"

It was the Duke Wellington answer at last.

He did not know whether with the roar and jangle of the train the business-blackmailer would actually have caught the words of his repeated defiance. But he knew that he must have taken it in.

The action had spoken as loud as any yelled-out word. The Duke Wellington answer.

He brought his right foot up beside his left, twisted himself around till he was butting up against the bare back of one of the last passengers to have scrabbled in, the old toy seller. He almost hugged the fellow in his effort to ensure his safety. The strong odor of his sweat struck pungently at his nostrils.

Above them both, the bright bundle of balloons bobbed up and down joyously, for all the imminent danger of being exploded by the nearest twirling fan.

At the next stop, Bombay Central, he got off. His mind still in turmoil, he wandered over the pedestrian bridge down into the main-line terminus and made his way, wrapped in increasingly down-spiraling thought, through the concourse, vaguely heading for home. Hardly anything he saw registered. An anxious clerk was attempting to amend the notice-board of the second-class reservation chart. There was the usual soldier with rifle and bayonet on guard outside the divisional pay office. A row of sleeping men on spread-out gunny sacks had high up above them a long line of identical posters one after another advertising a film with an English title *New Delhi*. But those two words did, curiously, impinge. He thought abruptly of his fellow blackmail victim, if at Freddy Kersasp's hands rather than Mama Chiplunkar's, Ramesh Deswani, who had jumped from the sixteenth floor of that new four-star hotel in the capital. Should not Ramesh Deswani have dared, instead of admitting in his suicide note to "serious mistakes," to give his tormentor the Duke Wellington answer?

But he found himself unable to pass judgment.

The thought had put fully back into his consciousness, however, what it was he had done himself. Yes, he had defied Mama Chiplunkar, as perhaps he ought to have done at the first mention of blackmail. But what would Chiplunkar be doing in face of that defiance? Perhaps even now? He imagined him as having turned away at once as soon as he had seen the man he had believed to be his pawn vanish away onto that speeding train. He would immediately have suspected a police trap and scurried and run to get out of it.

That notion gave him for an instant a dart of pleasure. It was high time Chiplunkar was made to run.

But darker thoughts swirled back. It would not have taken the brown-sugar kingpin very long to have realized there had been no trap, that there were no pursuers. And then . . . then he would at once have begun to think of taking revenge on this victim who had dared to defy him. More than sweet revenge, too, he would want to teach anyone he had forced to accept one of his business bargains that it was something they could not go back on.

So, as soon as he could, Chiplunkar would go to wherever it was he was hiding his wretched witness, Ranchod. Then he would take the fellow to some sycophantic police officer—he was known to have not a few of those, lavish as he was with whisky, women, tickets—to repeat his account of seeing this Inspector Ghote leaving Dolly Daruwala's flat in the wake of the man who had murdered her. And that would be the end of everything.

His own career would be over from that moment on, with only the grim process of an investigation by Vigilance Branch and subsequent disciplinary proceedings to be dragged out afterward. It would be terrible. But in a way it was deserved. He had deliberately committed an act that by the standards of the law and the courts was wrong. He had let—there could be no backing away from it—a murderer go free, even if he was a man who was an honor to the human race.

And now by one impulsive action, right though it may have been, he had betrayed that man to everything that earlier he had seen himself as saving him from.

The thought was almost unbearable.

Was this the time, after all, to do what Mr. Deswani had done in that Delhi hotel? To end it all?

Yet he found there was still something in him that put that dreadful last step out of the question. No, disgrace would come. Poverty, no doubt, would follow. And the acid remembrance of what he had done to a great man would be there forever in his mind. But he could not, for whatever reason, for no reason, plunge into that final dark hiding place.

He found that he had left the bustling terminus and had walked more than halfway home. He had even drunk one of the tiny glasses of milky-brown coffee served by the fellow who customarily squatted with his pail of the scarcely warm liquid just outside the big station. If he happened to pass that way he invariably stopped and bought a glass. In his earliest days in the city he had been told it was the best coffee in Bombay, and though he had since discovered this was patently untrue, the habit had persisted, if only for the pleasure of exchanging a familiar word. But had he actually drunk a glass just now, said a word, smiled? Or had he simply gone by unseeing? He could not remember.

Then, yet nearer home, he found that he had something almost as hard to bear as the depression that had flooded over him when he had first realized the full implications of his Duke Wellington answer. He had to go through the motions of living his ordinary life until the time Mama Chiplunkar chose to strike.

The time of waiting proved to be much longer than Ghote in his worst moments had envisaged. He had hardly expected that a team from Vigilance Branch would come gate-crashing into his flat on the very evening of his train escape from Mama Chip-lunkar's clutches. So that night he had managed to get through the hours until he could decently take himself off to bed without betraying—so at least he believed—too much of his anxiety. Mercifully, Ved as soon as they had eaten went around to the home of a friend until eight o'clock, the time Protima insisted he had to be back. So the subject of the home computer did not arise. But at work next day he found himself looking up from his desk every two or three minutes expecting to see the bat-wing doors of his office brushed aside by a hostile investigator.

However, the day wore on and no one appeared. By the time he was due to leave in the evening, he had worked himself into a state of terrible apprehension. Why had the blow not fallen? What was Mama Chiplunkar waiting for? He even found himself

thinking that for some inexplicable reason the brown-sugar
kingpin must have decided not to take his revenge. Then he
thought that perhaps he was delaying deliberately. The cat
playing with the mouse.

But his reason, asserting itself at last, told him that this was not
really very likely. Every hour that passed without Mama Chiplunkar making a move must increase the chances of police action
against him, even though he would take care now not to go
anywhere near the Multiplex Chemicals and Drug Manufacturing laboratory. In fact, he thought, it was more than likely that
instructions had gone at once to the in charge there to transfer all
the incriminating evidence to some place of safety. But the loss of
such a valuable asset as the laboratory would surely only have
increased Chiplunkar's rage, and his determination to pay out the
person he must believe had been responsible.

Yet nothing had happened.

What could Chiplunkar be doing? Could he have met with
some accident? Perhaps in hurry-scurrying away from Grant
Road station yesterday he had slipped and fallen onto the line.
Been killed. Been seriously injured.

But, no. Such miracles of luck did not happen. And besides, if
the Commissioner's current prime target had been swept from
the earth, the news would have been all over headquarters in no
time. Entire Bombay would have known even. Had the fellow so
much as been taken to hospital, word would have spread. Mama
Chiplunkar's name appeared in the papers often enough as one of
Bombay's prominent gang leaders and "social workers." Someone was bound to have recognized it, or him, and have run to a
telephone to tell some reporter.

Almost hoping that, after all, at this last moment of his
working day the blow would fall and the suspense be ended, he
gathered up his papers, locked them in his desk drawer, and went
to collect his scooter, left at headquarters the evening before with
his sudden decision to go to Grant Road station. Once again, as
the wretched machine proved the very devil to start up, he
thought of how, if he had been a different sort of officer, he
might even today be taking possession of a brand-new replace-

ment at Mama Chiplunkar's hands. Or of a car, even. One of those neat little Marutis. In return for services rendered. And to be rendered month after month, year after year.

What gifts, he wondered for the first time then, had that waddling old clerk constable, his predecessor as Mama Chiplunkar's headquarters goinda, received? Pretty small ones, no doubt. Business-business Chiplunkar would not have paid out one paisa more than he needed to.

And if that old bumbler had not had his heart attack . . . if he was still alive . . . still feeding Chiplunkar with his tip-offs . . . then would none of his own present troubles have existed? Perhaps not. But the thought of life free from the crouching weight of the business-blackmailer, now despite his Duke Wellington answer heavier than ever, of a once-again carefree existence, was too much even to think about. Tears rose up behind his eyes.

He gave his scooter one more violent kick, and the damn thing sprang at last to life.

Two more days went by with two evenings at home before them. On each of them he had thrust aside the tentative inquiries Ved had made and ignored the looks Protima had given him. They were evenings spent in ghastly imitation of the evenings there had been in the days before Mama Chiplunkar had first come up to him. And still nothing had happened.

At headquarters he could barely refrain from asking anyone he met whether they had heard anything about the Commissioner's target criminal. But he did not dare draw attention to himself. What if, by some unimaginable series of chances, his name was still not wholly linked to that of the gang boss? Perhaps then even the hint of an inquiry on his part would be all that was needed to set the dogs of Vigilance Branch on his heels.

And his work was suffering. He knew it. But he was simply unable to concentrate. There was a case he was meant to be working on—it had been with him, off and on, for months—the theft of an Arab visitor's jewel box from one of the big hotels in North Bombay. They had arrested the culprit weeks before. But there had been difficulties because the visitor had returned to the Gulf and was slow to answer inquiries. Now, however, all that was needed was confirming that every item of connecting evidence was ready. But, finishing for the day, it suddenly came over him that, lost in speculation about Mama Chiplunkar, he had totally forgotten to enclose something in the file. Yet his mind was blank. He had no idea at all what he had left out.

He had had to go back and sit at his desk in the exact position he had been in before. Then, in a last-second, merciful, sweat-flushing burst of illumination, he had remembered. It was the statements of the panches who had witnessed the search of the thief's quarters at the rear of the hotel. They were still in one of his desk drawers.

It was twenty minutes later as he was riding his scooter up to the compound gate—the bloody thing was jerking up and down beneath him as if it were some wild horse—that, above the bangs and judders it was making, he just caught his name shouted out aloud.

He looked around, throttling back a little.

And there, running toward him, frantically waving a hand, was Inspector Arjun Singh. Now of Vigilance Branch.

It has come at last, he thought. Yes, this is it.

He brought the scooter to a halt, nearly tipping it over in his anxiety.

He had never before, to his recollection, experienced the sensation of his bowels turning to water in alarm, not even when his life had been in actual danger. But now, with a gurgling rumble plainly to be heard with the shutting-off of the scooter motor, he became aware that something very much of this nature was taking place inside him.

Yes, he thought, they have been clever to put Singh on the job. He is knowing me. He has perhaps told them even that I have always been not quite able to take his aggressive manner. If they had any doubts, they will have calculated I would cave in to Singh before he had questioned me for one hour.

Well, I will not give them so much of satisfaction, he said to himself. I will just only fully admit right away that I have done wrong. And that will be the end of it. No shoutings and sneerings from Singh, no bullyings and browbeatings. At least I will behave with somewhat of dignity.

He braced himself.

Arjun Singh came up, broad, burly, head crowned with a massive, thickly bound pink turban, inescapably threatening.

"So, Singh sahib, it is you," he said.

He was relieved to hear his voice was steady, even manly. In spite of what was happening down in the region of his stomach.

"'Singh sahib'? 'Singh sahib'? What is this formality, bhai?"

The joviality of that did what he had promised himself no amount of hectoring would achieve. He felt all at once puny. If Singh was going to do it all in a friendly, we-were-colleagues-once way, he did not think he could bear it.

He felt within a tendency to weep, no less. To break down in sobbing tears.

He took a grip on himself. Dignity. Dignity. Would Dr. Commissariat grovel and blubber when it came to his turn? No, he would accept it, take it for what it was.

He squared his shoulders.

"So what is it you are wanting with me?"

"Wanting? Wanting? To say hello only. I have been seeing A.C.P. sahib, and coming out into the compound I heard a certain noise. At once I was saying to myself there is just only one thing in whole damn world making a racket like that: Ghote's scooter. So I called and chased, and here I am."

"It is that only?"

He could not help spilling out the remark.

"Oh, so you are not at all ashamed of the noise you are making each and every evening? Disturbing A.C.P. sahib in his cabin. Disturbing Commissioner himself even?"

"Yes. No. Well, yes. Somewhat I am ashamed, but . . ."

"But on our pay and allowances we are not going to be getting a scooter that is noiseless like a sewing machine, isn't it? Not unless we are taking big-big bribes, yes?"

Ghote smiled. A pale smile, but a smile.

"So what for were you seeing A.C.P. sahib?" he asked, for something to say.

"Oh, it is this Mama Chiplunkar business. They were remembering I had been on that fellow's tail before, and they were wanting to know if I am able to help now."

"What help?" Ghote said, mystified.

Arjun Singh laughed.

"You are not hearing what has happened to Mama?" he said, plainly incredulous. "Bhai, you must be only damn officer in whole of headquarters who is not knowing."

"But what has happened to him? What?"

Could it be that the fellow had after all been killed running from Grant Road station? Or been injured only? Badly injured?

"Damn scoundrel has gone to Ahmedabad," Singh answered. "They were keeping shadow watch on him, you know. And then one afternoon—it was three days ago, no, four—they were suddenly losing him. Afterward they decided he knew all the time the shadowing fellows were there, so when he was wanting for some reason to do something top secret he was simply giving them a slip. It was by God's grace only they were picking him up again. They spotted by chance. He was off to airport. Catching just only, five minutes to spare, plane for Ahmedabad."

"Ahmedabad?" Ghote repeated stupidly.

He could not think why Chiplunkar, evidently panicked because of what had happened at that meeting at Grant Road station, should have gone to the Gujarat city.

Singh soon enlightened him.

"Yes," he said, "nobody was knowing why Mama, who after all is from Konkan, a true Maharashtrian, should suddenly be off to Gujarat. But I was able to tell the A.C.P. Easy answer."

By now Ghote was almost completely back on an even keel. He was aware that the trouble in his stomach had ceased, too, as quickly as it had begun.

"So what easy answer were you giving, bhai?" he said. "Trust you to be one ahead in game always."

Singh gave a short appreciative laugh.

"Easy," he said. "The fellow has a mistress in Ahmedabad.

Sikh, I am sorry to say, though it was because of that I was hearing about the lady. Very much hot stuff. So, after all, Mama is just only having one little sex holiday. No more than that only."

But Ghote secretly knew better. No doubt now that Chiplunkar had panicked at Grant Road station. Had been panicked by him himself. And that panic had lasted till now, as was reasonable enough taking into account the information he had given the fellow when he believed he would not live to take advantage of it. So he had gone to ground. Gone to ground with his Sikh mistress, very hot stuff, somewhere where he had a nice little flat in distant Ahmedabad.

But for how long would he stay there?

SIXTEEN

Ghote's state of suspension, not relieved in the end by his encounter with Arjun Singh, continued next day almost unabated. Once more he fought to give to such work as he had on hand the concentration it required, and as time went by he even began to be more successful. Toward the end of the afternoon a whole hour passed, nearly, without him once thinking of the threat that hung over him. But then suddenly, for no apparent reason, it all came flooding back. That first visit from squinting Ranchod, the later, more urgent visits when the fellow had been drooling with the symptoms of drug deprivation, the terrible morning when as he had wrestled with his scooter Mama Chiplunkar had appeared at his side, to finally, their confrontation amid the straining, shoving home-going passengers at Grant Road station.

Then, as he was thinking it was nearly time to take himself back home, together with the threat of Mama Chiplunkar's revenge that hovered always over his head like a lightning-filled cloud, the doors of his office were suddenly jerked open. A peon he recognized as none other than the Commissioner's personal man stood there.

"Commissioner sahib is wanting to see. Now."

It was an order as swiftly to be obeyed as if the Commissioner himself had barked it out.

Ghote rose up from his chair.

He felt perfectly calm. It was as if, he briefly thought, he was some piece of rough, new-molded metal that had been placed on the first section of a long conveyor-belt. He would proceed now at a steady, unvarying pace, and at intervals something would be done to him. A jagged edge would be ground down. A different surface would be flipped over to be given a rapid polish. And eventually he would be spewed forth at the end of the process. Spewed forth as what? As, surely, a former officer of the Bombay Police, disgraced, humiliated, rejected.

He gave himself a quick look in his little square of mirror. Hair neat. Well shaved, thank goodness. But his shirt . . . it was his oldest one again, the green with the wavy black squares he had been so pleased to find he had in the office here when he had wanted to look inconspicuous in his attempt on Mama Chiplunkar.

Well, then, there was a sort of justice in the shabby appearance he would make now before the Commissioner.

He followed the peon out and through the compound to the squarely impressive entrance to the Commissioner's office building. With a gulp he climbed the wide stone steps outside, with their little, glintingly polished brass cannons to left and right. Once he had stepped across the threshold he became aware, with the sudden green and purple gloom that was all his eyes would register, that the sun outside had been beating down with its full force. No doubt sweat had sprung up all over his body in the short walk across. He would look even less smart than before.

But smartness no longer mattered. Or it would not do so in a very short time. A former police officer's appearance was altogether unimportant.

Directly in front of him, where the grand, red-carpeted double staircase marched magnificently up to either side, heavy brass rods gleaming at every step, he made out as his eyes grew accustomed to the comparative dimness out of the sun, the statue of Stephen Meredith Edwardes. Pattern of Police Commissioners of the British days, unswerving guardian of Bombay's peace, calm in white marble, epauletted, bemedaled. He straightened his shoulders.

Would that austere figure have thought for one moment of not returning the Duke Wellington answer to anyone who had dared to attempt to blackmail him? And what short shrift he would have given an officer of his who had had the unthinkable temerity to take the law into his own hands and let a murderer walk free?

Well, in two minutes only, he thought to himself, I would find out what today's Commissioner is thinking of such an officer. And I suspect it will not be so different from the opinion of Mr. Stephen Meredith Edwardes.

Behind the trotting peon he mounted the right-hand wing of the staircase. The somber oil portraits of the Commissioner's predecessors stared down at him.

At the top he presented himself to the havildar behind his little desk.

"Go in at once, Inspector. Commissioner sahib is waiting."

Again he pulled his shoulders back. The heavy double doors of the Commissioner's own office were in front of him, ten feet of dark carved wood. He pushed at them, aware at once that his hand had left a sweaty patch on the immaculately polished surface. The heavy leaves swung open to engulf him.

The Commissioner, formidable in uniform ironed and polished to the last degree, sat upright behind his enormous desk, the desk at which Commissioner after Commissioner had worked far back into the British days. Ruling the force. Keeping the peace. Maintaining discipline.

He marched across, came to a halt, and clicked heels sharply.

"Inspector Ghote, sir," he said.

His voice had not trembled, had not croaked.

"Ah, Ghote, yes. Now, listen. I was chatting this morning to Mr. Z. R. Mistry after our weekly conference, and—"

He stopped abruptly.

"Ghote," he said, "the doors are still an inch or two open. Shut them, will you?"

"Yes, sir, yes."

Ghote hurried back over.

How had he come to add this blunder to the tally of his wrongdoings?

Carefully he drew the heavy leaves together, heard the latch softly click, and turned around again to face the wrath to come.

But what could the Commissioner have learned from Mr. Z. R. Mistry? He himself, on that appalling night of Dolly Daruwala's death, had been careful to tell the Additional Secretary an outright lie about what had happened. He had said, and Mr. Mistry had plainly taken him at his word, that he had found Dolly Daruwala's body as soon as he had entered the flat. He had breathed not a word about Dr. Commissariat. So why was the Commissioner approaching the matter in hand in this way?

But no time to search for an answer now.

He crossed back to the huge desk and stood again at attention in front of it.

"Good," the Commissioner said. "Can't be too careful when security is involved."

But what security? Security had been broken the moment on the telephone at the paanwalla's stall he himself had muttered the words *Multiplex Chemical and Drug Manufacturing*.

"Now, Ghote, Mr. Mistry was telling me—I don't want to hear the ins and outs of it, mind—that you happen to be in possession of a set of keys to the flat in the Marzban Apartments building once occupied by a lady of unpleasant repute by the name of Dolly Daruwala. Correct?"

What was this? What did the keys that he had blackmailed that Muslim locksmith in Bapu Khote Cross Lane into making have to do with Mama Chiplunkar and the hold the brown-sugar kingpin had over himself?

"Yes, sir," he managed to get out in answer.

And, yes, he thought, he did actually still have those keys. After all this time. He had intended to dispose of them, as incriminating evidence, immediately after his illegal entry into Dolly Daruwala's flat. He had slipped them into the top pocket of his second-best uniform, the uniform Mr. Mistry had insisted on his wearing, and in the aftermath of the terrible event that had

taken place there he had forgotten all about them. And he had
not had occasion since to wear that uniform, rather than his best
one kept for court appearances and rare ceremonial occasions. It
had hung in its place in the almirah unwashed, unironed, from
that day to this.

But why was the Commissioner talking about keys?

"Now, perhaps you don't know—as I say, we've been keeping
security cent percent tight—that this flat at Marzban Apartments
was purchased some time after the Daruwala woman's death by
none other than our friend Mama Chiplunkar. Apparently he had
a need for somewhere unknown to most of his confederates, a
sudden need. What that was exactly we haven't discovered. But
the Intelligence wallas have found out definitely that the flat was
bought—black money transaction, needless to say—by Chiplunkar in person."

You may not know why he was buying it, Commissioner
sahib, Ghote said to himself with a tinge of triumph. But I can
have one jolly good guess. It must have been to keep Ranchod
safe inside, the one only threat Chiplunkar possessed to obtain
the services of a new goinda at headquarters.

But when would the Commissioner get around to Ranchod?

Or, could it be . . . It was too astonishing to allow himself to
think about. Could it be that this summons to the great man's
presence was not, after all, anything to do with Ranchod and the
blackmail that had begun with him?

"Now, Ghote, the point is this. Thanks to Inspector Arjun
Singh and his altogether excellent background knowledge of the
city's ne'er-do-wells, we have got Chiplunkar back in our sights
once more. In fact, we know he has booked a flight here from
Ahmedabad, where apparently he has some sort of love nest, for
today itself."

The Commissioner broke off and looked for something among
the few papers on the huge expanse of his desk.

Mama Chiplunkar coming back to Bombay, Ghote thought,
all his fears and troubles rushing back. Coming back today. And
what would be the first thing he would do? He would go to
Dolly Daruwala's old flat, pick up from there Ranchod, and take

him around to whatever friend he has at whatever police thana to tell his tale about one Inspector Ghote. Inspector Ghote who had dared to give him the Duke Wellington answer.

And it would not help at all that it was known now that the flat belonged to Chiplunkar. Even if they raided it as soon as the man himself had arrived from Ahmedabad and found him there with all the brown sugar and even the apparatus for making it that they could want, he still would be able to take his revenge. Ranchod would still be there. Ranchod's account of what happened at Marzban Apartments on the night Dolly Daruwala was stabbed to death would still be there to be told. His true account. And passing it on would doubtless still make things a hell of a lot easier for Chiplunkar, however much brown sugar was found in his possession.

So it was leadenly enough that he heard the Commissioner, who had at last found his note of what time the plane from Ahmedabad was due, go on to detail the plan to arrest Chiplunkar. It was exactly as he had begun working it out. Using those keys he still had, they would enter the flat as soon as possible. In it they would conduct as thorough a search for evidence as time permitted. Panches to witness it had already been notified. Then, as Chiplunkar stepped through the door, as he was likely to do very soon after his return from Gujarat, anxious to make sure the basis of his ill-gotten fortune was still intact, he would be nabbed.

"So where are those keys, Ghote?"

"Keys, sir? What—"

He pulled himself together.

"They are at my flat only, sir. It would not take twenty minutes to be fetching them."

"Good. First class. Take them straight to Marzban Apartments. You'll find Inspector Welankar there with a search party and the panches. This will be a good day for Bombay Police, Ghote. A damn good day."

Oh yes, Ghote said to himself as he carefully closed the two tall doors of the Commissioner's office behind him. Oh yes, for

Bombay Police it will be a damn good day. But for Inspector
Ghote . . .

For Inspector Ghote, whatever happened, it would be the
worst day of his life.

SEVENTEEN

Once again Ghote approached Marzban Apartments. The last time he had stood looking up at the tall tower block it had been at night when he had seen Mr. Z. R. Mistry leaving and had discovered that Ranchod was no longer in his employ. He had supposed then that the man was dead, another victim of brown sugar, and all the while—fleetingly he gave a rictus of a smile at the irony of it—all the while the fellow had been Mama Chiplunkar's prisoner in this very block. His counter in the evil game he was set on playing.

The time before that when he had waited, hiding in the shadows, he had been, despite his police uniform, intent on nothing less than housebreaking. And now once again here he was, not wearing uniform but in his oldest, green-and-black-checked shirt, which he had not dared to take time to change while he had dashed into his flat, run to the almirah, wriggled the two keys out of his uniform pocket, babbled something to Protima about "official business," and rushed away again.

Well, this would be the last official business it would ever fall to him to undertake.

So now, instead of climbing flight after flight up to that twentieth-floor flat as he had done the distant night when, little though he had known it, his lifetime career had entered its path to destruction, he simply took the lift. He pressed the neat button with the figure 20 lit up beside it and was swept smoothly and almost silently to his destination.

There, stepping out, he found the landing crowded almost to overflowing. Inspector Welankar had with him two sub-inspectors, four constables, and—he started with surprise—Mr. Framrose, his witness to Shiv Chand's attempt at blackmail, with the second panch for this operation, a nondescript, dark-complexioned man, probably some sort of southerner.

Somehow the unexpected presence of Mr. Framrose—only, it was not really so unlikely: he must have been noted as a useful panch at Shiv Chand's trial—filled him with a sense of unease. Perhaps it was simply because the old man was a Parsi, like Dr. Commissariat. There was another similarity about them, too, he thought. The aged panch had mentioned once—it must have been on their way to the court of sessions when his own mind was fighting back thoughts of killing Mama Chiplunkar—that, now he was retired, he prayed always for two hours a day. And, for all that prayer had not been part of his own life since his early boyhood, he had always felt a certain awe for those who sincerely practiced it. Yes, Mr. Framrose was, like Dr. Commissariat, though on a less heroic scale, a good man.

And now here he was himself about finally to betray Dr. Commissariat. There was nothing anymore to be done about it. The fatal step had been taken. It had been taken at that moment he had defied Mama Chiplunkar. But he found in himself now a new doubt about that sudden decision. Very well, it had been, in its way, a good action. It had given an evil man the courageous Duke Wellington answer. But it had also been—he felt it at this instant more keenly than ever—the betrayal of a man of goodness.

Should he, after all, have done it, he asked himself yet again. Could he not, somehow, have continued to pay Mama Chiplunkar his price? Cheating him where he could, withholding what he could when he could? And saving in the meanwhile a man who had made a great sacrifice for the sake of his fellow citizens? Who had made, really, two great sacrifices. First, in scorning the riches of America and coming to his native land with his life-giving invention, and second, in freeing from Dolly Daruwala's icy clutches all those she had had in her power.

But too late now. The conveyor belt he was on was rolling steadily forward. He had been put on to it, he had put himself on to it, and there was no getting off.

"You have brought those keys?" Inspector Welankar asked urgently.

Ghote drew them from his pocket.

"Then open up. Open up."

He stepped forward, slid the first of the keys into its slot.

The series of little scraping sounds it made as he pushed it home gave him a horrible sense of repeating an action he knew was going to lead him into a nightmare. Everything seemed, indeed, dreamlike. And as much filled with inexplicable menace as dreams often are.

But the key turned without real trouble, as it had done on the night Dolly Daruwala had died. Its fellow slid home more easily, as it also had done. And then the flat door was open, and Welankar and his men surged forward.

Inside it was all blackly familiar. On the small table in the hallway where Dolly Daruwala had been accustomed, foolishly, to drop her keys as she had entered, there was still the large creamy white fluted vase that, when he had been here before, had held a luxuriant display of flowers. It was nearly empty now, although drooping from it were some pale dried fronds. Could they be, he thought, the remains of the very flowers he had seen before? Yes, almost certainly they were.

He found his mouth had gone suddenly dry.

Brushed onward by Welankar and his men, he entered the drawing room. And again, it was all familiar. Eerily familiar. The big Amritsar carpet looked, perhaps, a little less flowerily bright than it had that night. Dust must in the weeks and weeks since then have settled on it undisturbed. A grayish film of it lay, indeed, on the low table where Dolly Daruwala had kept the big silver cigarette lighter that flouted Parsi principles. The lighter itself was no longer there. It was, after all, the sort of thing Mama

Chiplunkar would appropriate. But the copy of *Gup Shup* he had noticed that terrible night, and had nearly told the Assistant Commissioner that he had seen, was still lying where it had been, equally beneath a powdery layer of dust. Hardly what Mama Chiplunkar would choose to read, if he ever read anything at all. The cover of the television was lying on the floor beside the set, a sprawled mess. No doubt television had kept the brown-sugar kingpin amused at such times as he had stayed in the flat with his prisoner.

Had it amused Ranchod as well? And where in any case was Ranchod? He must be here. Why else would Mama Chiplunkar have allowed the flat to stay in this semideserted state? But there had been no sound out of the fellow. Perhaps he was crouching somewhere—under that green-covered bed in the next room?— hiding in fear at this noisy invasion.

Or had his own guess been wrong after all? Had Chiplunkar put his drug-addict prisoner into some other place? And would that mean that somehow the witness against him might never be brought forward?

No, he dared not hope it.

"Safe?" Welankar barked out, looking up from the tear-away search he and his men were making. "There must be a safe. The stuff would be in there. No sign of anything here."

Ghote nearly blurted out that the safe was actually in the bedroom beyond—its door was shut still—but just in time he remembered he was not supposed ever to have been in the place. Never mind how he had come into possession of keys to it.

But Welankar was already striding toward the bedroom.

Its door resisted him.

Ah, Ghote thought, Chiplunkar must have kept Ranchod locked up in there. And, yes, he must really be lying under that green bed, among all the dust rolls, shivering in fear.

Welankar was now throwing himself in a fierce shoulder charge at the locked door.

Well, Ghote said to himself, it will not resist for long. The woodwork in these posh flats is altogether rotten. I remember that from before. And when they are finding Ranchod inside, that will be the end itself.

Could he possibly get hold of the fellow before Welankar did? Take advantage of Welankar making first of all for the safe and the evidence of brown-sugar dealings he wanted? Haul Ranchod from under the bed and push him outside without anyone noticing? All right, then he would most likely become once again the man's blackmail victim. But that blackmailing had been curiously acceptable. Pleasant, even. A known routine.

But, no. No, it would be impossible to get the fellow out of the flat unseen. Mr. Framrose and his fellow panch, at least, would be bound to notice. They had been standing, he had been vaguely aware, just inside the drawing room door, like a pair of tethered and bewildered goats.

And somehow being seen with Ranchod by the good old Parsi would be a sort of unspoken condemnation. No, his downfall was there before him at the end of the conveyor belt, and there was no way of halting its progress.

Welankar had ordered the burliest of his search party to join him in battering at the locked door. And now, with a rending squeak, it gave.

Ranchod, it was at once evident, was not hiding under the shiny green cover of the bed. He was lying on the floor immediately under the open door of Dolly Daruwala's safe. Brown sugar in fearful plenty was scattered beside him. More smeared his outstretched hands. Yet more was still stacked in the safe above. And he was dead. Dead beyond all doubting, though not long so. Utterly overdosed.

They clustered round the distorted, convulsed body.

"This is one damn bloody complication," Welankar said.

To Ghote the implications were only slowly sinking in. For him, surely, Ranchod's death—the fellow must somehow have learned the combination of the safe where he knew Chiplunkar had stored the brown sugar from his laboratory—was far from being a complication.

But then, into the awed silence that the sight of the body had produced in everyone except Welankar, there came three sharp rings from the telephone in the drawing room.

"My God," Welankar said, "it must be Chiplunkar himself arriving downstairs. I told the chowkidar to give warning."

In a staccato burst of orders he told all but two of his men to remain in total silence in the bedroom, indicated to Ghote that he should stay with them, bundled the two panches in as well, and then positioned himself with his toughest constable just inside the drawing room where they could not be seen by anybody entering the flat. Ghote pushed the bedroom door almost closed, hoping its splintered lock would not be immediately visible.

They waited. At last from outside they heard keys turning in the door. There followed the sound of someone sibilantly whistling.

It grew nearer as Chiplunkar—if it was Chiplunkar—strolled through the hallway and stepped into the drawing room.

There was a muffled cry.

"Ram Chandra Chiplunkar," came Welankar's voice, "I am arresting you under Section Two-six-seven-A, Indian Penal Code, unauthorized possession of drugs."

And it was over, Ghote realized, a great wash of light breaking in on him. It was over, over, over. The unimaginable had happened. He had at times during his long nightmare toyed with thoughts of how some impossible piece of luck might pluck him to safety. But he had not for a moment really believed that would happen.

But it had. It had. And it had happened not entirely by a miracle. His own action had been the trigger for it. If he had not at last given Mama Chiplunkar the Duke Wellington answer, Chiplunkar would not have fled in panic from Grant Road station to his Ahmedabad hideaway. And then Ranchod would not have been left hour upon hour, day after day, locked in the bedroom of the flat here, locked in with that safe full of the brown sugar he craved. He would have not then worked at its combination till his guesses at the right figures, half-seen perhaps when Chiplunkar had hurried in to hide the stuff from his laboratory, had at last opened its door to him.

Yes, that was how it must have been. And it meant that the weight on him was, unbelievably, lifted. And more, he realized. The black boulder that had loomed on his horizon ever since he had witnessed Dr. Commissariat dealing with that vermin, pest, and snake Dolly Daruwala in this very room had vanished away as if it had never been. He himself, and he alone, now knew that good man's secret. No one was going to believe Chiplunkar if he tried to repeat Ranchod's story of what he had seen on the stairs that night, nor had he the least trace of proof to back it up with.

And he himself would keep the secret deep sealed in an ever-locked chest within himself. The great scientist was safe. He himself was safe. It was over, over, over.

He was already waiting at home when Ved came back from playing cricket—he was vice-captain now of the Regals—but he did not even take time to ask him how the game had gone. The moment Protima unbolted the door he spoke.

"Ved, I have been thinking only. I am sure it is one first-class idea for you to have home computer. Do you think that one will have gone by now?"

A huge smile broke out on Ved's face.

"No, Dadaji, no," he said. "It is still definitely available. I was telephoning gentleman in question as soon as I was seeing you would in the end decide in favor and saying yes. Yes, we would buy."

Ghote did not know whether that was blackmail or not. And he did not care.